This igloo book belongs to:

. . . .

Published in 2012
by Igloo Books Ltd
Cottage Farm
Sywell
NN6 0BJ
www.igloobooks.com

SHE001 0912
10 9 8 7 6 5 4 3 2 1
ISBN 978-0-85780-760-1

Illustrated by Robert Dunn, Roger Langton and Sara Silcock
Stories retold by Joff Brown

Printed and manufactured in China

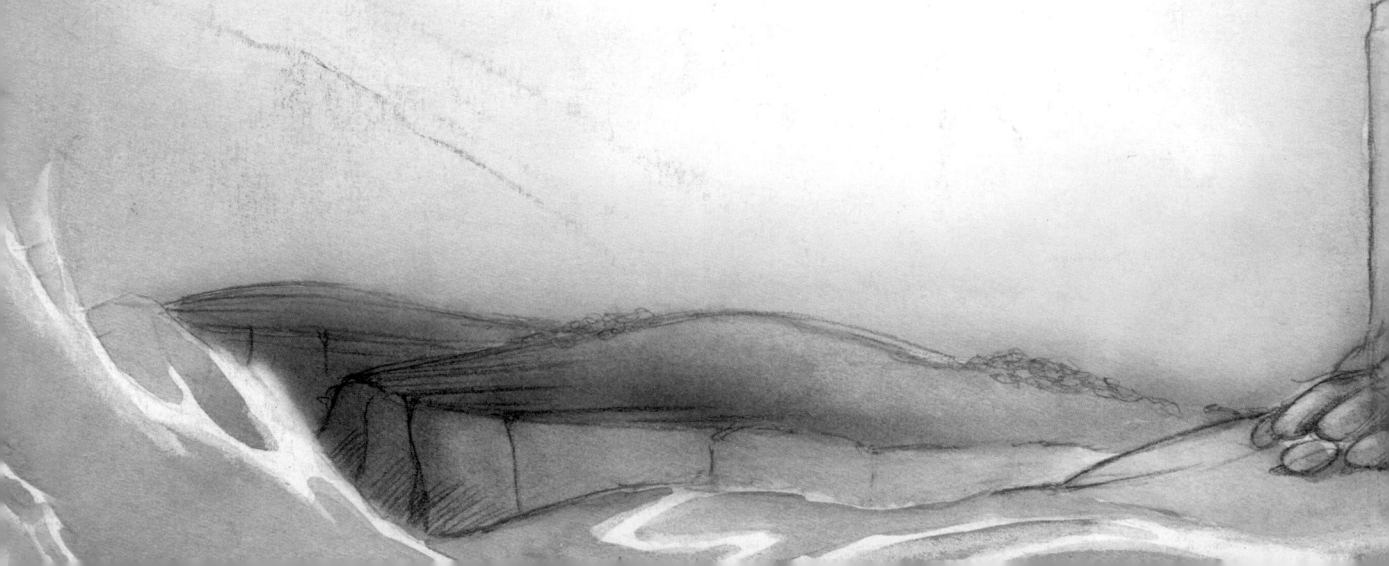

Knights
and
Dragons

igloobooks
.com

Contents

The Dragon Egg . . . . page 6

The Clockwork Knight . . . . page 14

The Knight and the Dragon . . . . page 22

The Cockatrice . . . . page 30

The Tinder Box . . . . page 38

The Blacksmith's Blade . . . . page 46

The Sprites and the Dragon . . . . page 54

The Sword in the Stone . . . . page 62

The Dragon and the Thief . . . . page 70

The Sorcerer's Apprentice . . . . page 78

The Cowardly Dragon . . . . page 86

The Sea Serpent . . . . page 94

The Knight's Tower . . . . page 102

The Troll Knight . . . . page 108

The Fire Dragon . . . . page 116

The Jester's Quest . . . . page 122

The Knight of the Golden Lion . . . . page 130

Sir Richard and the Red Knight . . . . page 138

Sir Gawaine and the Green Knight . . . . page 146

The Ice Knight . . . . page 154

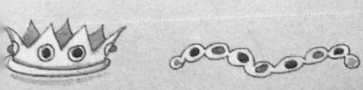

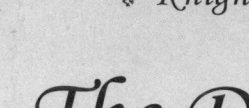 

The Dragon Egg

Once upon a time, two dragons were out flying when they were caught in a terrible storm. They were blown far from their home in the mountains.

The two dragons were parents of an egg that the mother dragon was carrying in her claws. Suddenly, a huge bolt of lightning shot from the sky, hitting the mother dragon. With a terrible shriek, she dropped the egg. It fell below the storm clouds to the ground, far below. When the storm ended, the dragons searched all over the land for their egg, but they couldn't find it.

"Dragon eggs are stronger than steel," said the father dragon. "We may still see our child one day."

Deep in the valleys, a young man called John lived on a small farm with his mother and father. On the night of the storm, there was a terrible crash, but John slept right through it. However, in the morning, when he woke up, he found a hole in his ceiling and an enormous object at the end of his bed. "I wonder what it is," thought John. He didn't know it was the lost egg.

John was just taking the big egg outside when he felt something moving inside it. He dropped the egg in fright. The eggshell cracked and a head poked out. Suddenly, a bright red, young dragon crawled out of the eggshell. When the dragon saw John, it bounded over to him, knocked him over and licked his face, just like a dog.

John took the dragon to show his parents. "I'm going to keep the dragon as a pet," he said.

But keeping a dragon wasn't that easy. When it sneezed, it spat out a burst of flame! When the young dragon flapped its wings, it nearly smashed everything in the cottage! The Dragon began to get bigger, day by day, until the red dragon was larger than John himself!

"I know you like the dragon," said John's parents, "we can't keep it here." "It'll never survive if we turn it loose." said John. "I'll take it back up the mountains where the dragons live. Maybe it can find its parents there."

John's father took a big piece of the dragon egg to the blacksmith. The blacksmith could barely bend it, even in the white heat of his forge. However, eventually he managed to shape it into a shield. John's father gave his son the shield. "This will protect you from enemies," he said.

John and the dragon set off on the long journey out of the green valleys, towards the mountains. The higher they got, the colder it became, but every night John kept warm by sleeping next to the dragon, who had a belly as hot as a furnace!

They followed a winding path through the fields and into a deep forest, until they reached a dead end. The storm had blown down a huge tree across their path and there was no way across. John tried to hack at the tree with his trusty axe, but it was too big to break. He was about to give up, when he saw the young dragon sucking in its breath. John jumped out of the way, just in time to avoid the dragon's fiery breath. It turned the tree to ashes in seconds and the way was clear again.

The path to the mountains began to curve around steep crags and deep, dangerous chasms in the earth.

Sometimes, they had to cross tiny, rickety bridges. It wasn't long before they came to a crevasse so deep, it seemed bottomless. The rope bridge across the crevasse creaked and twisted as they crossed it. The dragon was too heavy for the bridge and when John and the dragon were halfway across, the bridge snapped.

John fell screaming into the crevasse. He was expecting to hit the icy ground below, when he felt claws on his shoulders. Slowly, he began to rise. The dragon was flying and pulling him up.

When they reached the other side of the crevasse, John thanked the exhausted dragon, but it was busy sniffing the air. Suddenly, it ran off, towards a mountain covered in deep caves.

John tried to follow the dragon but suddenly, a great shadow fell over him. He looked up to see a huge, green dragon. The dragon roared when it saw John and blew an enormous jet of fire at him.

John raised his dragon egg shield and it protected him from the fire, but the green dragon roared again and tried to bite him. John swung his axe bravely, but he thought he would soon be eaten.

Suddenly, John heard a smaller roar. It was the young, red dragon! It flew up to him with a much larger red dragon at its side. When the green dragon saw them, it stopped attacking John. Instead, it flew to the young, red dragon and nuzzled it affectionately.

"The big, red dragon and the green dragon must be its parents," thought John. Even though he was very scared, John followed the dragons back to their cave.

"I'm sorry for attacking you," said the green dragon. "Thank you for rescuing our child. Take this treasure as a reward." The dragon pushed a glittering pile of jewels and gold towards John. However, John was so worn out that he couldn't even thank the dragon. He just collapsed on the pile of treasure and fell fast asleep.

When John woke up, he found he wasn't in the cave any more. He was back at his mother and father's cottage. The great, green dragon had flown John all the way home on its back while he slept. It had bought the gold and jewels in a sack around its neck, too.

John said goodbye to the dragon, who flew back up to the mountains to join the dragon mother and their child.

The red dragon grew to be a mighty monster, but it never forgot John and often flew down from the mountains to see him. With their share of the dragon's treasure, John and his family lived happily ever after.

 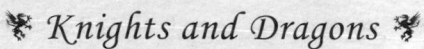  

The Clockwork Knight

Once upon a time, there was a poor toymaker who had one son and no daughters. The toymaker made wonderful toys such as wind-up dolls that walked, wooden dragons that roared and puppets that seemed almost real. But the toymaker sold his toys for so little that he and his son hardly had enough to eat.

One day, the toymaker's son, whose name was Peter, heard about a great treasure inside a huge fortress guarded by a dragon. It was many days' journey away. "I must go and find the treasure," said Peter. "Then we will no longer be poor."

"Before you go," said the toymaker said, "I will make you a companion who will keep you safe from harm." The toymaker toiled in his workshop for many days. With his last pennies, he bought sheets of brass and made them into arms and legs. He took clockwork wheels and made them into a clockwork heart and mind. He took a brass helmet and beat it into the shape of a face. When he was done, he had created a knight made of clockwork, as big as Peter. The knight moved stiffly, but he could walk and talk and even fight with his brass sword.

Peter and the clockwork knight set out on their journey.

At the end of the first day, they camped on stony ground. "Go to sleep," said the clockwork knight, "And I will watch for danger." The clockwork knight did not need to sleep and he guarded Peter all night.

The next morning, Peter wound up the clockwork knight with the big key in his back and they set off again. As they were travelling through a rocky pass, they were attacked by two long-eared, long-nosed trolls. The clockwork knight drew his gleaming brass sword and struck the trolls down before Peter could even move.

"Thank you for saving me," said Peter. "You are a brave companion." The clockwork knight bowed stiffly.

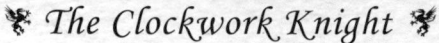

Peter and the clockwork knight continued their journey for many days, until they came to a fortress with a wide moat all round it. From a window in the very highest tower, Peter could see the glint of gold.

"The treasure is inside," said Peter. "How can we get across the moat? I can't swim."

"Neither can I," said the clockwork knight. "But maybe I do not need to." Without another word, the clockwork knight walked into the moat. Because he was clockwork, he needed no air to breathe. So, he was able to walk across the bottom of the moat and come out the other side.
Then he let down the draw bridge so that Peter could walk across.

Inside the castle, a mighty dragon guarded the gateway that led to the tower and the treasure. It was an ugly dragon with great fangs that curved down past its gigantic jaws.

Peter grabbed his sword. "It's time for me to fight the dragon," he said, nervously. "Wait," said the clockwork knight. The knight whirred all the cogs and gears of his clockwork mind to work out a way to get past the dragon and soon, he had an idea. "Master," he said to Peter, "When you see that the dragon is distracted, run to the gateway."

Before Peter could reply, the clockwork knight ran up to the dragon, brandishing his sword. When the dragon tried to grab the clockwork knight in its claws, the knight did nothing. Instead, he let the dragon bite at his brass body with its long fangs. "Run up the stairs, Master!" called the clockwork knight.

But Peter could see that the dragon was damaging the clockwork knight. With a great yell, Peter ran at the dragon and swiped his sword at the dragon's belly. Howling in pain, the dragon dropped the knight and flew off into the sky, far into the distance.

Peter knelt by the clockwork knight. The knight was dented and scratched and his legs were so bent that he could hardly stand.

"Why did you save me?" asked the clockwork knight. "You could have run through the gateway and got the treasure."

"You saved me from the trolls and you crossed the moat for me," said Peter. "You're a true friend, and friends don't leave each other behind."

Peter helped the clockwork knight up the stairs to the room at the top of the tallest tower. Treasure was piled in big heaps – emeralds, sapphires, rubies and all kinds of golden chains, crowns and bracelets. In one corner, there was a great fireplace filled with fierce flames.

"You will have to leave me here," said the clockwork knight sadly, "My legs are too bent to carry me home."

"Perhaps," said Peter, looking at all the gold, "and perhaps not." That night, Peter melted all of the gold in the fierce flames. He hammered it into the shape of legs and then took the clockwork knight's old brass legs off and then fixed the golden legs to the knight.

"Try them," said Peter. The clockwork knight stood up. He moved his new golden toes, then his golden feet, then his golden knees. He found that he could walk, hop and even run! He did a funny clockwork jig for joy. "My new legs are perfect," said the clockwork knight, "now we can go home."

Peter and the knight gathered all the treasure that they could carry. They journeyed for many days, all the way back to the toymaker's house and the clockwork knight kept watch over Peter every night, his golden legs gleaming in the moonlight.

When the toymaker saw them returning with the treasure, he ran out of his shop and hugged them both. "We will never be hungry again," he said.

As a reward for his hard work, the clockwork knight was polished until he shone and his clockwork heart swelled so much that it almost burst out of his brass chest. And Peter, the toymaker and the clockwork knight lived happily ever after.

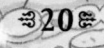

The Knight and the Dragon

A long time ago, a Lord and Lady had a son named John. John hated work of any kind and loved lazing around in the meadows outside the town. He never helped his parents when they visited the local townspeople. He would always find an excuse to stay home.

One Sunday, John pretended to be ill so he could avoid work and spend all day playing in the woods. As John was climbing a tree, he saw a strange-looking snake curled around a branch. The snake had red scales and sharp little teeth. John picked up the snake, but it tried to bite him.

"This snake might be dangerous," thought John. "I should take it home and cage it, so that it can't cause any trouble." But the snake was too slippery to hold, so John threw the snake down a nearby well. "I'm sure it can't hurt anyone down there," he thought.

Years passed and the snake in the well grew bigger and bigger.
It grew scales and horns and great feet with claws as big as knives.
And the sharp teeth also got bigger and bigger too. Soon, the snake wasn't a
snake any more, it was a dragon!

One day, the dragon crept out of the well and snapped up insects and
birds. As it grew even larger and larger, it started eating rabbits, then deer,
until it was sneaking into fields and stealing sheep.

One night, it curled its long body around a hill behind the local town and went to sleep. When the townspeople saw the dragon the next morning, they were terrified. They marched to the manor house and banged on the door. "You must save us from the dragon!" they cried.

When the dragon awoke it slithered down to the manor house. Puffs of flame shot from its nostrils and a hiss-like steam came from its gaping jaws. When the townspeople saw, they banged on the manor house's door. A sleepy butler unlocked the great door and was surprised when all the townspeople rushed in, slamming the door behind them. The dragon howled and stamped outside in a rage.

The lady of the manor had a clever idea. She asked the townspeople to run to the dairy and pour all the day's milk into a deep trough. When the dragon saw the milk, it drank it all up and looked around for more. When it saw there wasn't any more, it roared and crept back to its hill to sleep.

Every day from then on, the dragon drank all the town's milk and slept, but it still ripped up meadows, knocked down houses and scared the sheep and cows. Many knights and heroes came to defeat the dragon, but the dragon always won.

Meanwhile, John had become a great knight. When he retuned home and his parents told him about the dragon, he looked out at the dragon's hill. He realised that the dragon was the snake he had found all those years ago.

John's parents told him all about the heroes who had failed to defeat the dragon, but John knew what to do. "This is a special type of monster," he said, "and it will need something special to defeat it." He spoke to the town's blacksmith and asked him to make him a new suit of armor with some very unusual parts.

The next day, the forge in the town rang with the sound of steel, as the blacksmith made the special armor. Nobody had ever seen armor like it before. It had spikes jutting out of it at all angles. When it was complete, John put it on—he looked a fearsome sight.

Clanking and creaking, John walked to the dragon's hill. He waved his sword and shouted at the dragon. The dragon raised its ugly head and roared, then slid off the hill.

John marched towards the dragon, shouting all the time. Quick as a flash, the dragon wound its body around John. John swiped his sword at the dragon's head, but it was too fast for him. He couldn't hit it at all.

The dragon began to squeeze and squeeze, but the spikes on John's armor dug into it, hurting it. The harder the dragon squeezed, the more it hurt. Instead of running away, or using its fearsome flames, the foolish dragon just kept on squeezing.

The battle continued all day, until the dragon was so tired and hurt, that it uncoiled itself and slithered away, never to return.

The townspeople were overjoyed. They were safe at last. John became a hero and everyone lived happily ever after.

The Cockatrice

A long time ago, in a sleepy village, there was an old abbey by a river that had stood empty for many years. Nobody went near it, and some of the villagers even said it was haunted. The only living things that wandered into those dark ruins were the ducks and geese from the river.

One day, a duck laid an egg which rolled into a dark, dank hole in the ruins. The hole led to the crypt, the space under the abbey that was filled with old tombs. The egg lay there until a fat toad hopped along and sat on the egg until it hatched.

When a toad hatches a duck's egg, especially in such a dark and mysterious place, something very strange happens. When the egg hatched, out came a small, scaly creature like a dragon. Its wings were covered in green feathers, but it had four scaly legs and a long, whip-like tail. Its head was a little bit like an ugly bird's, but its eyes gleamed bright red, like hot coals. It was a cockatrice.

The cockatrice lived in the crypt of the abbey and ate all the small creatures it could find, until it grew to the size of a crocodile. Then it started to come out of the crypt at night, to look for bigger animals to eat.

Soon, the villagers told tales of a strange dragon-like creature that stole sheep from the fields. It wasn't long until a shepherd was found in the middle of a field one morning, standing still and cold. He had been turned to stone by the cockatrice's gaze.

Now the villagers became very scared. They wouldn't go out at night in case they saw the cockatrice's red eyes and got turned to stone themselves.

The mayor of the village offered a large plot of land to anyone who could kill the beast. It wasn't long before everyone was thinking how they could win the land and become a hero. "They say cockatrices can't kill weasels," said one villager.

"Nonsense!" said another. "Everyone knows that a cockatrice will die if it hears a rooster crow."

The only man in the village who didn't seem bothered about the cockatrice was Tom Green. He was a glassmaker who spent all his time making delicate ornaments, panes of glass for windows and mirrors. "I'm sure the cockatrice will go away in time," he said.

But the other villagers tried everything they could to defeat the monster. One villager collected weasels and let them loose down the hole. The legend was true and the weasels seemed immune to the cockatrice's evil glare. But the cockatrice simply ate up all the weasels, until there were none left.

One brave man even took a rooster down to the cockatrice's lair. The villagers heard it crow, but then they saw the man run out of the lair as fast as he could. "The beast turned the rooster to stone!" he panted.

Soon, many knights came to the village. They put on their heavy armor and picked up their great swords. Then they climbed down into the dark crypt where the cockatrice lived, but none of them ever came out again.

Things went from bad to worse, until nobody would come and visit the village at all and Tom found that nobody wanted to buy his glass either. There were no travellers to buy his ornaments and the villagers boarded up their windows to stop the cockatrice looking in, so they didn't need any window glass.

"I've had about enough of this cockatrice!" thought Tom. "I'm going to get rid of it, once and for all."

When Tom told the villagers that he was going to slay the cockatrice, they laughed at him. "You're just a glassmaker" they said. But Tom had a plan.

He spent weeks and weeks making the largest, best mirror he could. It was so big, Tom could only just carry it. It had a large hook on the top.

When the mirror was finished, Tom took his rusty old sword, the mirror and a piece of rope. He lowered the mirror into the cockatrice's lair. "If I can get the cockatrice to stare at its reflection," he thought, "it will turn itself to stone."

Tom sat at the edge of the hole and waited until he heard the cockatrice slithering up to the mirror. But when it looked at the mirror, the cockatrice didn't die because it was immune to its own deadly glaze. Tom Green was about to pull the mirror out and run away as fast as he could, when he noticed a curious thing. The cockatrice was hissing and spitting at the mirror. It opened its beak-like mouth and started scratching and butting the mirror.

"It thinks its reflection is another cockatrice," thought Tom. He held the mirror while the cockatrice swiped and clawed at it. Tom almost dropped it, but he held on as hard as he could. The cockatrice fought its reflection for many hours, until it was completely exhausted. With a giant sigh, the cockatrice fell back. Its deadly eyes were closed and it could hardly move.

As quick as a flash, Tom jumped down into the cockatrice's lair. It was filled with statues of warriors. "Those must be the knights that the cockatrice turned to stone," thought Tom.

The cockatrice heard Tom approach and roared. It began to twitch its eyelids, but before it could open its eyes, Tom struck it with his rusty old sword. As soon as the sword touched the creature, its body turned to stone.

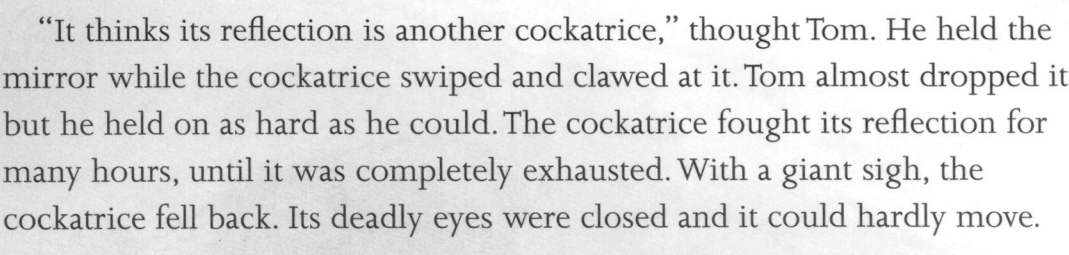

When the villagers heard the news, they rejoiced. The mayor gave Tom the plot of land and he built a fine new glassworks on it. People came from miles around to buy his glass models of the cockatrice and to hear him tell the story of how he defeated it.

The stone cockatrice was put on top of the abbey and stayed there for many years, until it crumbled to dust. But, even now, nobody in the sleepy village will keep ducks, or eat their eggs just in case one of those eggs hatches into another deadly cockatrice!

The Tinderbox

Once upon a time, a soldier was returning home from war when he met an old witch. "How would you like to have as much money as you want?" asked the witch.
"I would like that very much," said the soldier.

"Then go down the hole in this tree and you'll find a cave with a door at the end. Open it and you will see a dog who guards a chest full of copper coins. Look around and you will see another door. Behind this is a second dog who guards a chest of silver coins. Next, you will see a third door. Go through it and you will find a dog who watches over a chest of gold coins. If you pick these dogs up and put them on my blue apron, they won't harm you and you can take as many coins as you like."

"How much of this money will be mine?" asked the soldier, amazed. "All of it. I just want a little old tinderbox that my grandmother left down there. It's a small box with a flint inside, for lighting matches and it is guarded by the third dog."

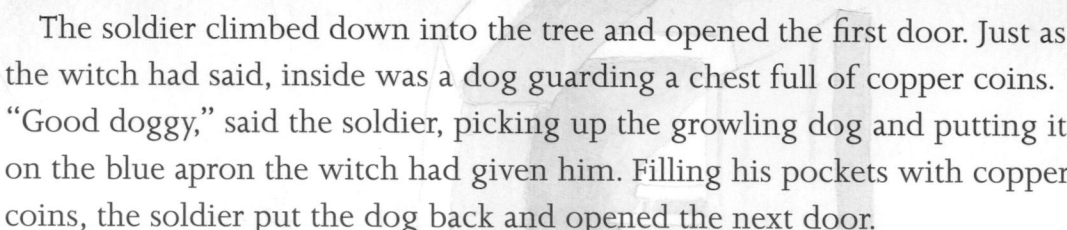

The soldier climbed down into the tree and opened the first door. Just as the witch had said, inside was a dog guarding a chest full of copper coins. "Good doggy," said the soldier, picking up the growling dog and putting it on the blue apron the witch had given him. Filling his pockets with copper coins, the soldier put the dog back and opened the next door.

Inside this room was a second dog who guarded a chest full of silver coins. Plucking up his courage, the soldier grabbed the dog and put it on the blue apron, then he grabbed handfuls of the silver coins.

Opening the door to the last room, the soldier found a third dog, which guarded a chest full of gold coins. It snarled and slobbered, but the soldier picked it up and put it onto the apron. The fearsome dog sat quietly while the soldier filled his remaining pockets with gold. The soldier found the little tinderbox, then made his way back to the hole in the tree .

The witch pulled the soldier out of the hole in the tree and asked for the tinderbox. "Why do you want it?" asked the soldier.

"Just give it to me!" screamed the witch and rushed to attack him, her fingernails like daggers. But the soldier was too fast for the witch. Before she could reach him, he drew his sword and chased her away.

Then soldier walked on until he reached a city. With all the money from the hole in the tree, the soldier was rich. He stayed in expensive rooms, bought the finest clothes and food and soon he had made a lot of new friends.

In the middle of the city was a palace. "A princess lives there," said his friends. "It has been foretold that she will marry a common man. But her wicked father, the king, keeps her locked in the palace."

The soldier bought so many expensive things that soon he had hardly any money left. He was forced to leave his rich lodgings and stay in a draughty old attic and all his new friends deserted him.

One cold day, the soldier decided to light a fire. He struck the old tinder box to get a spark and the brown dog appeared!

"What is your bidding, my master?" the dog growled. The soldier was delighted. "Bring me some money," he said and the dog ran off and in a flash returned with a bag of copper coins.

The soldier found that if he struck the tinderbox once, the first dog appeared and if he struck it twice, the second dog appeared. Striking it three times brought the third dog. Soon, the soldier had all the money he could spend again, but all he wanted was to meet the princess. So, that night he commanded the first dog to bring her to him. The dog ran off and reappeared with the princess on his back. She was very beautiful and he kissed the astonished princess' hand before asking the dog to return her.

"I had such a strange dream last night," said the princess at breakfast the next day. When her father the king heard what had happened, he grew suspicious. A serving-maid was sent to watch over her sleep.

The next night, the second dog brought the princess to the soldier. The serving-maid saw the dog take the princess to the soldier's house and she marked the door with a chalk cross.

The next morning, she took the king and queen down to the door. "She went in this house," she said. But all the houses had chalk crosses on! The clever dog had marked every house in the neighbourhood with chalk crosses to confuse the king and queen.

On the third night, the queen tied a bag of flour to the princess' dress. The soldier sent the first dog to bring the princess, but he didn't notice the bag spill flour. The king and queen followed the trail of flour to the soldier's house and had him arrested. The soldier was dragged to prison without his tinderbox.

The next day, the soldier was due to be executed. He called through his prison bars to a passing boy. "Please bring me my tinderbox." The boy brought it and when the soldier was on the scaffold and about to be executed, he asked the king for one last thing. "Could I have one last smoke?"

The king agreed and the soldier brought out his tinder-box and struck it once, twice, three times. The three dogs appeared and chased the wicked king and all his soldiers out of the city. The soldier was free and so was the princess. The soldier married the princess and became king of the city and they lived happily ever after.

The Blacksmith's Blade

Once upon a time, there lived a blacksmith's son called Leon. Leon longed to be a knight more than anything else in the world. While the knights from the great castle on the hill galloped off to go on quests, or fight in mighty tournaments, Leon had to stay at home and help his father make horseshoes, swords and nails.

One day, a tall, proud-looking man came to the blacksmith's workshop. "Make me a fine sword," he said, "and make sure you pour this liquid onto the iron as you do." The man handed Leon a bottle of strange, green liquid. "I will return for the sword next week," said the stranger and galloped off on his great black steed.

Leon worked for days on the sword. He rubbed the green liquid into the iron. Then he spent hours hammering and beating at the sword until it was the finest he had ever made. He held it up to the light, outside the workshop. "It is almost too good to sell," said Leon.

Just then, wicked bully chased some frightened children past the workshop. Suddenly, Leon felt the blade move in his hand, as if it was alive. He ran after the bully and stopped him with the flat part of the sword. The children thanked Leon for saving them, but the bully was enraged. "This man attacked me!" he cried. The bully called the town guards and Leon found himself taken before the king.

The king banished Leon so he left the kingdom in disgrace, with the sword as his only possession. "This is all your fault," Leon said to the sword. "I wish I'd never made you," and he raised his arms to throw the sword away.

"Wait, master!" said a high, sharp voice. It was the sword itself speaking! "I am an enchanted blade," it said. "If you find me a gold sheath to carry me in, a leather grip and a diamond for the end of my hilt, I will serve you well."

"Very well," said Leon. "After all, you're the only friend I have."

Then the sword told Leon to go high into the mountains. There, Leon saw a mean-looking goblin sleeping on a rock. The sword suddenely seemed to come alive in Leon's hand. It prodded the goblin awake. Leon was very scared, but the sword fought off the goblin, leaving only a beautiful gold sword-sheath behind. The sword slotted neatly into it.

"Now journey into the woods," said the sword. Deep in the heart of the forest, Leon saw a gang of robbers. They had just robbed a merchant and tied him to a tree with leather straps. The sword stirred in Leon's hand again and fought off the robbers. Leon untied the thankful merchant. "The robbers have run off with my treasure," the merchant said, "so I have nothing to give you." But Leon took the leather straps and tied them around the handle of the sword.

After many days' journey, Leon reached the mouth of a cave. Inside, lived a great and terrible dragon. "We will find a diamond inside," said the sword. Leon's knees were knocking and his teeth were chattering, but he entered the cave.

The dragon sat guarding an enormous mound of treasure. A fine, bright diamond twinkled in the middle of the hoard, just below the dragon's chest. "Burrow under the treasure and you will not be seen," said the sword.

Leon pushed his way under the mound of treasure until he reached the diamond. Slowly, he grabbed it and tunnelled his way out again. "Grab a handful of gold coins, then run!" said the sword, and Leon dashed out of the cave with the gold and the diamond. He was far away over the hills before the dragon saw that some of his treasure had been stolen.

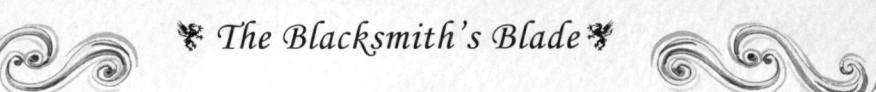

"Now I have my sheath, my grip and my diamond, said the sword, I will repay your kindness," and he gave Leon the dragons gold. With the dragons gold, Leon bought a suit of armor and a great white horse. "You must return to your home," said the sword, so Leon rode all the way back to the kingdom.

When Leon reached the kingdom, he found that a great tournament was being held there and the winner of the tournament would marry the King's daughter. "Enter the tournament," said the sword. Nobody saw that it was Leon in his shining armor and he was able to enter the tournament as a knight.

With the help of the enchanted sword, Leon fought knight after knight. He always managed to knock them down and win every battle. Soon, the only knight left to fight was one riding a black horse. They faced each other on the battleground, while all the people of the kingdom watched.

Suddenly, Leon felt the sword move in his hand, but this time, it didn't attack the knight. Instead, the sword flew out of Leon's hand and into the other knight's hand. The knight raised his visor and Leon saw that it was the man who had asked Leon to make the enchanted blade.

"This sword is mine," cried the knight. "And you're nothing but a blacksmith." He galloped towards Leon waiving his sword, ready to chop off his head. Leon turned to run, but there was nothing he could do. The other knight was too fast.

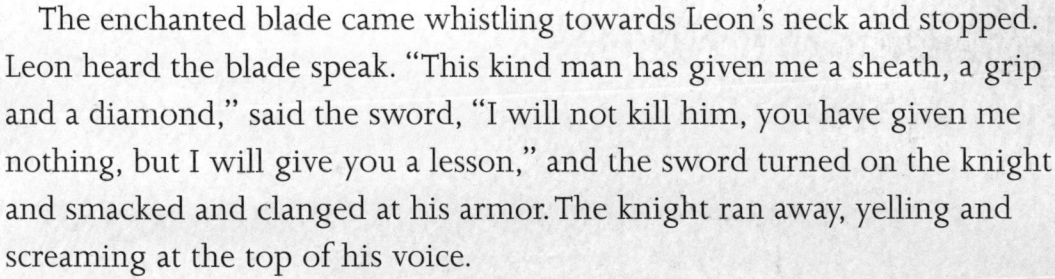

The enchanted blade came whistling towards Leon's neck and stopped. Leon heard the blade speak. "This kind man has given me a sheath, a grip and a diamond," said the sword, "I will not kill him, you have given me nothing, but I will give you a lesson," and the sword turned on the knight and smacked and clanged at his armor. The knight ran away, yelling and screaming at the top of his voice.

The people cheered and the king pronounced Leon the winner of the tournament. "You have won with kindness, not strength," said the King. Leon married the princess, and they all lived happily ever after.

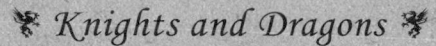

The Sprites and the Dragon

Once upon a time, a grim, old dragon lived in a cave high in the mountains. This dragon was almost as ancient as the mountains themselves. Once his scales had been deep bronze, but now they were greenish and faded. He was lean and scaly and his eyes glowed red like coals on a fire. Every animal for miles around was scared of the dragon.

The dragon had a pile of treasure, that he loved to sit on top of. It filled up his huge, echoing cave and was full of helmets and weapons from defeated knights, shimmering jewels and thousands of gold coins.

One gloomy day, the dragon was counting his jewels when he heard a high, chattering sound. Something small, green and giggling came into his cave. It was a skinny wood-sprite from the forest. "Let's live here now!" piped the sprite and suddenly, a whole crowd of sprites came pouring into the dragon's cave.

Nothing the dragon could do would get rid of the dancing, chattering sprites. And being shadowy little things, they couldn't be swiped with his claws or burned with his fiery breath. Every day, more and more sprites appeared, until the dragon couldn't sleep at all.

"Why are you here?" he asked the sprites. They told him that they had been chased out of their forest home by wolves. "We will live here, now," they squeaked," which made the dragon snort flames in surprise.

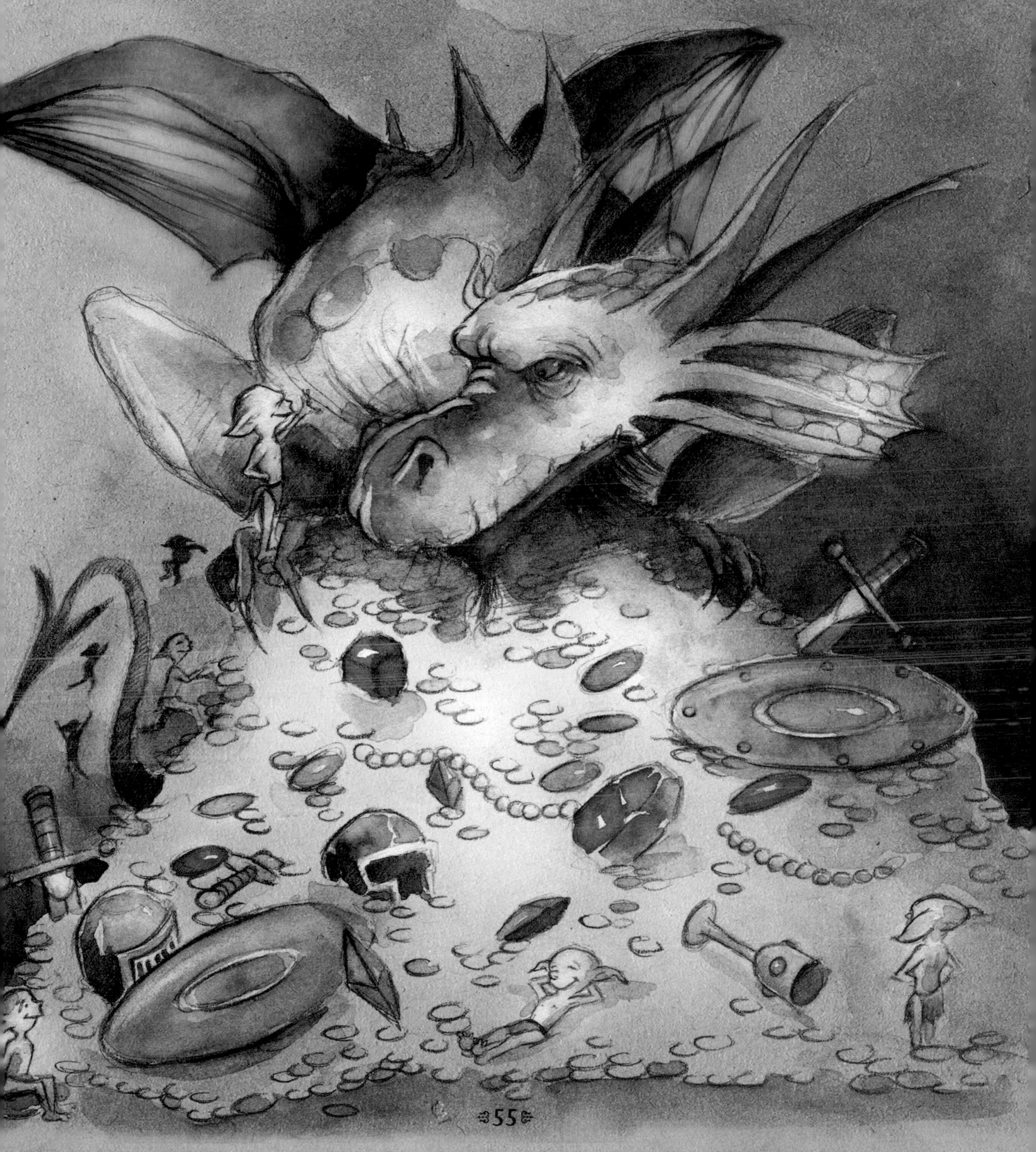

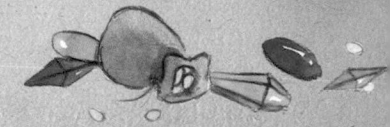

The next day, the dragon could take no more. He flew down from the mountains like a storm cloud, all the way to the forest. He searched for the wolves, but he was too big and they were too quick and clever for him. All he could see was their yellow eyes, staring at him from between the trees.

In a clearing, the dragon a woodcutter. The woodcutter was terrified and tried to run, but the dragon landed in front of him. "Tell me, woodcutter," roared the dragon. "Why do the wolves chase things out of this forest?"

"Because they want it all to themselves," replied the woodcutter. "We used to hire men to drive them away, but robbers took all our gold and nobody will help us now."

The dragon snorted and flew away, leaving the poor woodcutter trembling.

On the edge of the forest, the dragon found a family crowded into a tiny cottage. The mother and father shrunk back in fear when the dragon poked his long head through their door, but the children laughed and reached out to touch his snout.

"We have no fence, so the wolves came and stole our sheep," said the father. "They have eaten all the sheep and we are afraid we will be next."

The dragon snorted a second time and flew away, thinking.

On a high hill, the dragon saw a man dressed in battered old armor. This man didn't run away when the dragon landed. "I am a knight," said the man bravely. "If my armor was new, I would try to slay you and the wolves. But all my armor is rusted and useless."

The dragon snorted again and flapped slowly back to the mountains.

"If I get rid of the wolves in your forest, will you leave?" said the dragon to the sprites. The sprites said that they would.

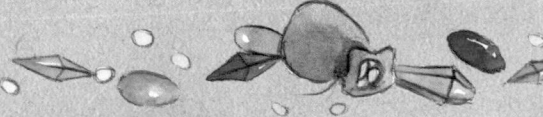

The next day, the dragon flew back down to the forest and dropped something at the woodcutter's feet. It was a huge, red ruby from his pile of treasure. "Sell this to find men to drive the wolves away," said the dragon.

Then the dragon spent an hour slashing at some tall trees with his claws, until he had a huge pile of wood which he bought to the farmer and his family. "Use this wood to build a strong fence to keep the wolves out," said the strong dragon.

Lastly, he flew back to his cave and picked up the toughest, shiniest armor, sword and helmet he could find. He brought it to the knight. "Wear this, but don't fight me," said the dragon. "Use it to drive the wolves away."

"I will if you will help me," said the knight.

So, the knight darted into the deep forest and chased the wolves out and

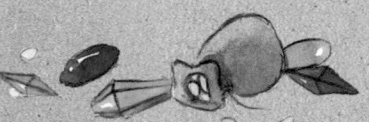
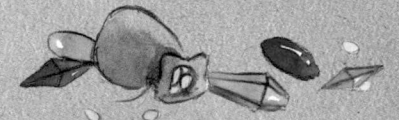

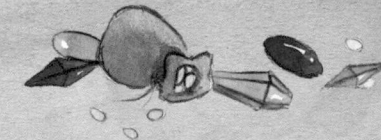

the dragon blew flames at them until the wolves scampered away in fright.

Later, the dragon visited the shepherd and his family. They had built a strong fence in case the wolves returned. "Now we're safe," said the farmer. "But we have no sheep. I don't know how we'll survive."

So, the dragon picked up wild sheep from the mountains in his great claws and dropped them into the fenced field. The shepherd and his wife thanked him, but the dragon was already flying back to his cave.

"The wolves are gone," said the dragon to the sprites in the cave. "Now leave!"

The sprites cartwheeled down the mountain and into the forest and the dragon sat down to guard his treasure in silence.

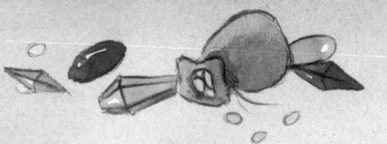 

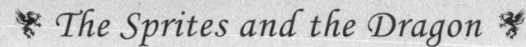

But something wasn't right. It was too quiet. Try as he might, the dragon couldn't get comfortable. What was the point of all his treasure he thought, if it didn't do anyone any good?

So the dragon flew back to the forest and was glad to see that the woodcutter, the farm family, the sprites and even the knight cheered when they saw him again. "You all need protecting more than my treasure does," rumbled the dragon. "And perhaps I was a little lonely in my old cave."

So, the dragon stayed in the forest. He carried his treasure down from the mountain and buried it deep under an oak tree. But when the people of the forest were in need, they sometimes found a great ruby on their doorstep, or an ancient gold coin lying in their fields as if it had been dropped there by the dragon.

They say that the dragon still guards the forest. So if you ever go into a forest and hear a sound like a fiery snort, or see a glint of bronze, don't worry; it's just the dragon, protecting you from the wolves.

The Sword in the Stone

Along time ago, a knight called Sir Ector lived in a great castle Sir Ector had two sons. The older one was named Kay and the younger one was called Arthur. Kay was training to be a knight. Arthur would work as Kay's squire.

While Kay learned all the skills of knighthood, Arthur had to clean Kay's armor, feed Kay's horse and do anything that Kay asked. At dinner, Kay got to sit at the head of the table with Sir Ector, while Arthur was made to sit far away at the other end. Sir Ector was a good man, but he didn't understand that Arthur was leading a miserable life.

One day, while Arthur was trying to polish Kay's suit of armor with an old rag, when he saw an old man who seemed to have appeared from nowhere. The man had a long, white beard, a set of dusty blue robes and a tall blue hat. "How can I help you, old man?" asked Arthur. "I am your new teacher," said the old man, with a mysterious smile. "I am a wizard and my name is Merlin."

From that day on, Merlin taught Arthur something every day. Because Merlin was a wizard, his lessons were never dull.

One day, Merlin turned Arthur into a bird, so he could learn wisdom from the owls deep in the woods. The next day, Arthur became a dog and learned how to command sheep in the fields.

"Why are you teaching me these things?" asked Arthur. "I am going to be a humble squire when I grow up aren't I? "But Merlin would just smile kindly and change the subject.

A year and a day after Merlin had arrived, Arthur went to his teacher's room and found that Merlin had packed up all his things. "I am leaving," said Merlin. "I have taught you everything you need to know." "Don't go!" said Arthur. "I still have so much to learn."

Merlin shook his head sadly. "You are ready now," he said "For what?" asked Arthur, but Merlin wouldn't say.

"I will return one day," Merlin said, "but for now, remember my advice when you are in need of a sword, look in a churchyard." Suddenly there was a crack and a flash of light and Merlin was gone.

Now, as it happened, there was no ruler in the kingdom where Arthur lived. The knights were always fighting amongst themselves and the only thing that brought them together was a competition, each year, to try and pull out a mighty sword that had become mysteriously stuck in a huge stone in the churchyard.

Each knight wanted to be the one to win the competition because the words written on the huge rock said, "Whoever pulls the sword out of the stone shall be King."

Every knight tried to pull the sword from the stone, but it was stuck fast.

Soon, the time came for Arthur's brother, Kay to try and pull the sword out of the stone, like every other knight. However, no matter how hard he pulled, the stone would not move.

"May I try?" asked Arthur, but Kay pushed him away. "You're not even a noble knight," said Kay.

The next day, there was an important tournament. Arthur carried Kay's armor on foot, while Kay rode on horseback. On the way, Kay realised that he had forgotten his sword. "Go back and get it for me," he told Arthur. "And be quick, or I will not be able to fight."

Arthur hurried back to their lodgings, but the house was locked. Everyone was at the tournament.

"What shall I do?" thought Arthur. And then he remembered Merlin's advice. "I must try to find Kay a sword," he thought. So he went into the churchyard where the sword sat in the stone. He pulled the sword and it came out of the stone as easily as a knife is pulled out of butter. Arthur rushed to Kay. "Here," he said. "It's not your sword, but will this one do?"

Kay took one look at the sword and gasped. "It's the sword in the stone!" All the other knights gathered round, forgetting about the tournament. "It's a trick!" they cried. "There must be a mistake. This boy isn't even a knight."

So Arthur, Kay and the rest of the knights returned to the churchyard. Arthur put the sword back into the stone and all the other knights tried to pull it out again. No matter how hard they tried, it wouldn't move. But when Arthur grasped the sword, he removed it from the stone as easily as the first time.
Sir Ector stepped forward. "Arthur, I have something to tell you," he said, gravely. "You are not my son. Your father was Uther Pendragon, King. Before he died, he asked me to adopt you, to keep you safe."

"Hail Arthur!" cried Ector, and all the knights got down on one knee and bowed to Arthur. Even Kay bowed down.
"I am sorry I treated you so badly," said Kay. "Now you are King, I expect you will banish me from your kingdom."

Arthur took Kay's hand and raised him up. "No, Kay," he said. "You are still my brother. You must become one of my knights. I will have a large, round table made, so that wherever my knights sit around it, they will all feel equal."

So Arthur became King. He had many legendary adventures with his knights of the round table and sometimes Merlin returned to give him advice, wisdom and just a little magic!

The Dragon and the Thief

Once there was a young man called Simpkin who was always in trouble. When he wasn't stealing apples from the orchards, he was cheating at games. When Simpkin wasn't frightening the cows in the field, he was tying bells to cats' tails and letting hens out of the henhouses.

Eventually, the king got to hear about Simpkin and all the trouble he was causing. So he sent his royal guards to bring Simpkin before the royal court. The king was very bad-tempered and everyone in the kingdom was afraid of him. If there was one thing the king disliked, it was young men making mischief and he was determined to punish Simpkin.

"You have been so wicked for so long," said the king, that we are going to cut your head off as punishment!"

Simpkin was very frightened. "Is there nothing I can do?" he asked. "Nothing," said the king. "Unless, maybe there is one thing. You know the horrible dragon who lives in the huge old castle on the hill?"
"The one who owns the flying horse and who breathes fire on anyone who comes near?" said Simpkin.

"Yes, that one," said the king. "Well, that dragon wants to be human. He stands on two legs, eats dinner at a dinner table and even sleeps in a feather bed. Next, he'll want to be king and we can't have that, now, can we?"

Simpkin shook his head obediently "No, your majesty."

"If you fetch me the dragon's flying horse, I will let you go free," said the king. So Simpkin set off for the castle. He sneaked into the gloomy, silent stables and found the magnificent winged horse. When he tried to untie it and ride it away, the horse let out a loud neigh.

The dragon in the castle heard the winged horse neighing. It stuck its scaly head out of the window. "Be quiet, beast!" it growled and went back to sleep.

Simpkin tried to take the horse away again, but it neighed even louder. The dragon woke up and this time it came down to the stables. Simpkin hid as fast as he could and watched as the dragon roared and growled at the winged horse, until it cowered and trembled in fear.

When the dragon had gone, Simpkin tried to take the horse again. This time, the horse was more than happy to get away from the frightful dragon.

Simpkin, being a very mischievous young man, jumped on the horse's back and flew right up to the dragon's bedroom window. "If anyone asks you who took your horse, tell them it was me, Simpkin the Magnificent!" shouted Simpkin and he flew away before the dragon could reply.

At the palace, Simpkin presented the flying horse to the king. Just for a moment, the king was very happy. "Am I free to go?" asked Simpkin.

"Wait!" said the king. "You must do one more thing. Fetch me the dragon's bedsheets."

Simpkin returned to the castle and climbed up the high walls. He found a small window and lowered himself down into the dragon's bedroom. He tiptoed quietly across the floor and reached out to grab the sheets. But when he pulled them, he found that they were covered with hundreds of little silver bells that tinkled and clanged. The sound woke the dragon up.

"Stop hogging the sheets!" the dragon yelled to its wife. It pulled the sheets down and Simpkin found he was in bed with the dragon!

When the dragon saw Simpkin, he was enraged. He tied Simpkin up and stowed him under the bed. "We will eat him tomorrow in a stew," said the dragon to its wife.

The next day, when the dragon was out flying, the dragon wife heated up the oven and was about to put Simpkin in a big pot. "You'd better take off these ropes," said Simpkin, "or they'll make the stew taste horrible."

So the dragon wife untied Simpkin. As quick as a flash, Simpkin jumped out of the pot and pushed the dragon wife into the fiery oven until she was cooked. Then he ran upstairs, grabbed the sheets and ran back to the king with them. "Now can I go?" asked Simpkin.

"No," said the king, who was really very cruel. "Now you must fetch me... the dragon itself!"

"Very well," said Simpkin. "But I'll need to grow a beard first."

The king agreed, although he didn't know what Simpkin was up to. Once Simpkin had waited weeks and weeks for a beard to grow on his chin, he set off for the dragon's castle for a third time. On the way, he met a beggar and asked him to change clothes with him. The beggar and Simpkin changed clothes and soon Simpkin arrived at the castle.

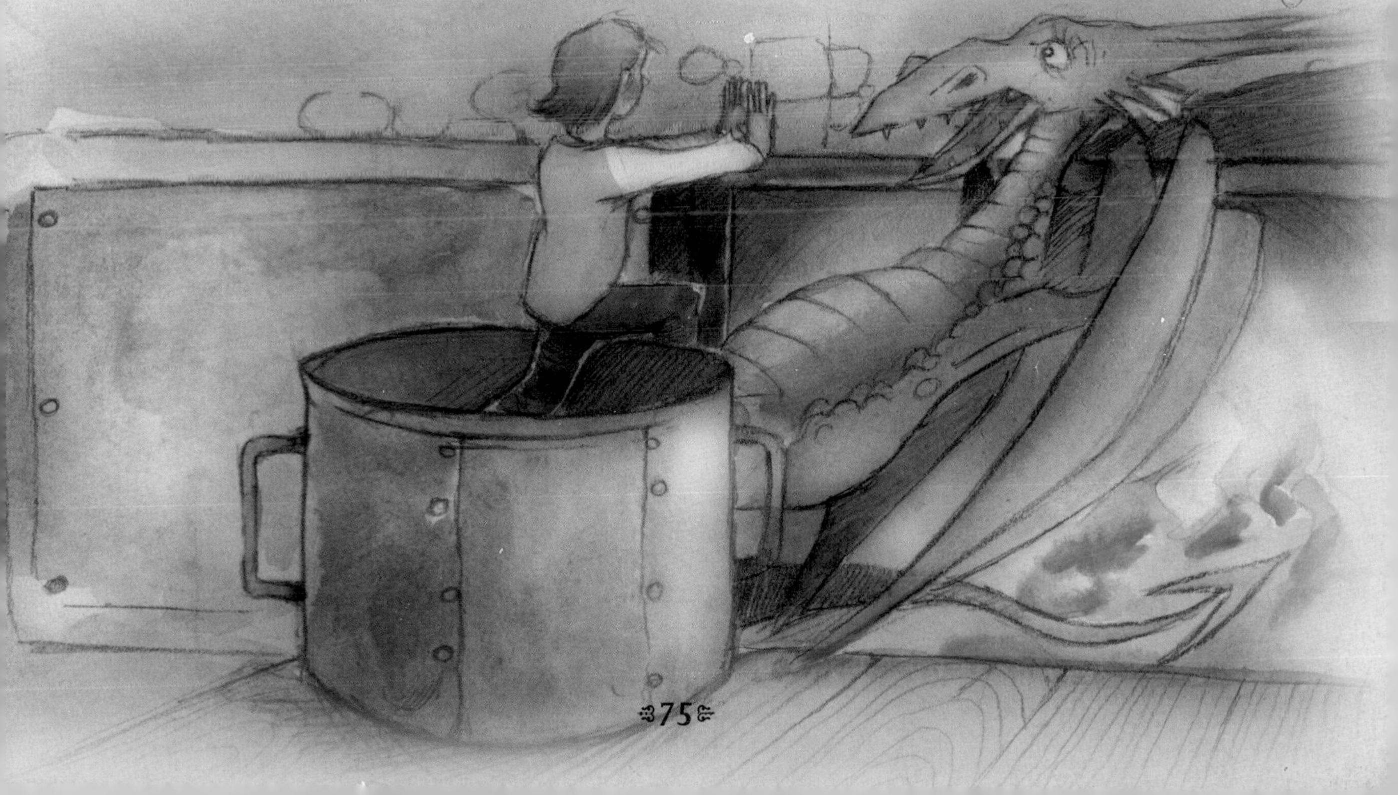

He knocked on the great door and the dragon answered. He didn't recognise Simpkin in the beggar's clothes. "Spare a penny for a beggar, sir?" asked Simpkin.

"Go away!" roared the dragon. "I'm building a big box to trap my enemy, Simpkin the Magnificent." The dragon showed Simpkin a large, sturdy box he was building.

Simpkin thought fast. "It's not big enough," said Simpkin. "I know and he's a big, tall man. He won't fit in there."

"Nonsense," said the dragon. "The box is so big, I could fit in it."

"I don't believe you," said Simpkin.

The dragon climbed into the box "Look!" he said, "there's plenty of room." Simpkin slammed the lid of the box shut and sealed it with heavy chains. Ignoring the horrible roars from inside the box, he dragged it all the way back to the king. "Now let me go free," said Simpkin.

"I don't believe the dragon's in there," the king said.

"See for yourself," said Simpkin. "Look, there's a big hatch in the side of the box. Open it and look in."

The king opened the hatch, which was too small to let the dragon out. But it was big enough for the dragon to squeeze his head out, grab the king in his huge jaws and swallow him whole!

Everyone in the kingdom was happy that the wicked king was dead. They asked Simpkin to be their new king and he accepted gratefully. As for the dragon, Simpkin kept it in the box as a pet. So Simpkin really did become Simpkin the Magnificent and he lived happily ever after.

The Sorcerer's Apprentice

Once there was a young boy who was apprenticed to a powerful sorcerer. The apprentice wanted to learn all the magic that he could so that, one day, he too would be as powerful as the sorcerer himself. The apprentice worked hard for the sorcerer for one year, but during all that time, the sorcerer didn't teach the apprentice a single spell. The apprentice spent his days washing the floors of the sorcerer's drafty castle and cleaning the glass containers that the sorcerer used to mix potions in. Sometimes, the leftover potions would mix together with a 'pop', or make an especially bad smell, or even form a laughing face from smoke that soon drifted apart. But this was the nearest the apprentice ever came to magic.

"Master, when will I learn to do magic like you?" the apprentice asked, one day "Maybe I could conjure up a little fireball. Or learn to fly, maybe? Just a little way off the ground?"

"Magic is about hard work and study, not flights and explosions," the sorcerer replied, locking his spellbook safely in his cabinet. "You're here to learn real magic, not stage tricks. Now, get back to work." The sorcerer was a very grave and stern man and the apprentice was a little afraid of him. So the apprentice carried on with his cleaning, but he still longed to cast some real spells.

One day, the sorcerer told the apprentice that he would have to go away for a few days and while he was gone, he wanted the Great Hall cleaned.

The apprentice looked around the Great Hall in dismay. The floor was encrusted with grime. There were dirty cauldrons and dusty glass beakers piled up everywhere. Even the stuffed animal heads on the wall were covered in cobwebs. It was going to take a long time to clean.

The sorcerer departed and the apprentice found a mop and filled a pail of water from the well outside. He began to scrub one corner of the floor, rubbing all the dirt off and making it shine. After an hour or two, he stood up and stretched his aching back. He had only cleaned a tiny part of the floor. The rest was as dirty as ever.

The apprentice left his mop and wandered around the workshop. He was surprised to see that his master's cabinet was unlocked. Peering inside, he saw the sorcerer's spellbook. He was not allowed to touch the spellbook, or even look inside it because it was the source of all the sorcerer's power.

"A small look can't hurt," thought the apprentice. He took the spellbook from the cabinet and opened it. It fell open on a page with a spell that made household objects move around. "Hmm," thought the apprentice. "I wonder if the mop could do the sweeping for me."

The apprentice recited the words on the page loudly, pointing at the mop. At first, nothing happened. Then the mop shook and picked itself up from the floor. It began scrubbing the floor all by itself. It even slid back to the pail of water and dipped itself in, before returning to its task.

"Fantastic!" cried the apprentice out loud. He pulled up a chair and watched as the mop scrubbed away at the floor. Soon, all the water was gone from the pail, but the mop kept scrubbing away.

The apprentice thumbed through the spellbook and found a spell that made water appear. He cast it on the bucket and instantly it was full to the brim with water and suds.

It wasn't long before the mop had cleaned the whole floor to a sparkling shine. But the mop didn't stop. It went back to the first corner and started cleaning again. The apprentice looked in the spellbook, but there were no instructions on stopping the spell. The mop began to clean faster and faster. It started to swipe at the objects on the long tables, knocking over all kinds of magical equipment.

"Hey! Stop that!" cried the apprentice. He chased the mop around the hall, until he finally grabbed it with both hands. He snapped the mop in two. "That's the end of that," he said.

However it wasn't! The two halves of the mop began to grow and sprout, until there were two full-sized mops instead of one. Both mops rushed around the hall, swiping and smashing.

Then the apprentice noticed that his feet were wet. The spell on the bucket was making water pour out of it. It was filling up the room. The apprentice grabbed a hammer and chased the two mops, smashing them to bits. But all the splinters of the mops grew and grew until there were a hundred mops flying through the air.

The water grew so high, the apprentice had to swim. He tried to fight off the mops, but they were everywhere, slashing and swiping and destroying everything in the hall. "If only my master were here!" cried the apprentice in fright.

Suddenly, there was a crack of thunder and a blast of light as the sorcerer appeared. With a wave of his arms, he made the water disappear and with a click of his fingers, the mops fell to the floor and turned back into a single, lifeless mop.

"Please don't turn me into a toad," begged the apprentice, who was still soaking wet.

"I left the cabinet open to see if you could be trusted," the sorcerer said. "I knew you would be meddling with magic as soon as you opened my spellbook, but I didn't return until you had seen what wild magic can do."

"I'm so sorry, Master," said the apprentice. "I'll never dabble in magic without your permission again." The sorcerer made the apprentice clean up the mess with his own hands, but that was all the punishment the apprentice got.

After many years' of hard work, the apprentice became a mighty sorcerer. But he never forgot the lesson that his master had taught him that day.

The Cowardly Dragon

Deep in a forest, there lived a cowardly dragon. He was as big as ten elephants. He breathed fire and had long claws. But the dragon was scared of everything. When he saw a mouse, he jumped in the air. When he heard an owl hoot, he shivered. He was scared when he went to sleep on the ground in the forest, in case any wild animals jumped out at him.

One day, the dragon was sniffing flowers when he heard a loud noise. It was a group of children playing in the wood. The dragon hid behind a hill and listened to them, his heart pounding. "I've never met a child before," thought the dragon. "What if they're dangerous?"

Just then, the children ran around the hill and saw the dragon sitting there. The dragon was so scared, he let out a terrible roar that echoed all the way through the forest. All the children ran away in fear, except one. Instead of running, the boy shouted back, "Yaaaah!"

The dragon was so frightened that he started to cry. "Please don't hurt me," he said, in his deep voice. "You look very dangerous."

The little boy went up to him and took the dragon's claw. "I was only joking," said the boy. "My name is Tristan. Come and play with us."

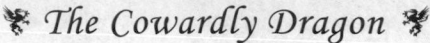 

Tristan took the dragon to meet his other friends. At first, the dragon was too shy to speak to them, but soon they were all playing happily together. Tristan was the bravest of them all. There was no tree too high for him to climb, no hill too rocky for him to scramble up and no stream too cold to swim in.

"How can I be like you?" the dragon asked Tristan. "You're not scared of anything."

"You just need a friend to give you courage," said Tristan. "Why don't you come back to town with me? You can stay at our house."

"It sounds scary," said the dragon, but Tristan tugged on his claw and took him all the way back to the town.

"Shhh," said Tristan, as they entered the town. "The mayor doesn't like any noise." So the two friends tiptoed down the street. But the dragon's claws clattered so loudly on the cobblestones that everyone came out to see what the noise was. "Don't worry," said Tristan to the townspeople, who were as frightened as the dragon. "He's my friend."

Tristan persuaded the dragon to meet his mother and father. "You are welcome to stay," said Tristan's father. "I am a farmer and my haystack will make a comfy bed for you."

So the dragon went to sleep in the haystack, which was far more comfortable than the cold, hard ground in the forest. "Maybe these people aren't so scary after all," he thought.

The next day, the townspeople had a street party to welcome the dragon. The town's baker baked hundreds of delicious cakes for the party. When lunchtime came, all the cakes were put out on long tables in the town square.

"You must meet the mayor," said Tristan. "Nobody likes him, because he has forbidden children from playing in the streets. But you must be polite to him, because he is the most important man in town."

The mayor was a short, cross-looking man with a big gold chain around his neck. The dragon was so nervous about meeting such an important person that he was shaking all over. When he stretched out his thumb and forefinger to shake the mayor's hand, he shook so much that he accidentally knocked the mayor over. The mayor looked even angrier. "It is very rude to be so large," huffed the mayor. "Please try not to make a mess."

The baker lit the candles on the cakes. "Blow them out," Tristan said to the dragon. The dragon took a deep breath and blew on the candles, but a huge flame came out of his mouth and burned all the cakes to cinders.

"I'm sorry," said the dragon. Everyone was furious with him.

"I spent all morning baking those cakes!" shouted the bakers.

It was too much for the dragon. He sat down with a mighty thump and started to cry. The tears from his eyes sprayed out like a rainstorm and, within moments, the entire town square was wet. Some people put up umbrellas, but most of the townsfolk were drenched.

"I've had enough of this nonsense!" shouted the mayor, stamping his foot. "Tristan, you brought this monster to our town and now you must be punished! I order you and your family to leave this town and never come back!" All the townspeople gasped, but they were too frightened of the mayor to say anything. Tristan was so shocked, he started to cry, too.

When the dragon saw Tristan crying, a strange thing happened. The dragon got so angry, his enormous tears dried up. He even forgot to feel afraid. He stood up to his full height, towering over the people of the town. He stamped over to the mayor and picked him up in his claws. Suddenly, the mayor didn't look so frightening after all.

"How dare you talk to my friend like that." boomed the dragon. "You should be ashamed of yourself, picking on a little boy! You're nothing but a bully!"

And before the mayor could reply, the dragon threw the mayor up in the air and batted him away with his tail. The mayor flew through the air and landed on Tristan's father's haystack. He was so frightened, he ran out of town and never came back.

With the mayor gone, the children could play in the town as much as they wanted. The people of the town gave the dragon a huge shiny gold medal. The dragon was so happy, he decided to stay in the town with Tristan and they lived happily ever after.

The Sea Serpent

Once upon a time, a gigantic sea serpent lived near many islands. The serpent was as big as ten dragons. Its eyes were the size of lakes and each of its teeth was as high as a tower. When it raised its head above the water, it made huge waves crash into the cliffs of the nearby islands. And when it roared, everyone could hear it for miles around.

One day, the king of one of the islands looked out and saw that the waves crashing by his cliffside castle were much higher than usual. He watched as the great sea serpent raised its head out of the water, until its eyes were as high as the king's tower. The king leaned out of his castle window and shook his fist at the sea serpent. "Be gone, foul beast!" he cried. But the serpent let out a roar that almost shook the castle apart.

The king sent out his chief wizard to see if he could enchant the sea serpent away, but the old wizard was powerless. The serpent roared at the wizard, who ran back to the castle before the sea serpent could eat him up.

This wizard was a very wise and clever man who could understand the speech of sea serpents. When he spoke to the king, he trembled almost as much as he had done when he had seen the sea serpent. "Sire," said the wizard. "The sea serpent is angry at your insult to it. It says he will only go away if he is given your only daughter to eat. If he does not have her, he will destroy your castle."

The king was scared, as well as angry now. However, he made his heralds ride all over the island with a proclamation; "Anyone who can kill the sea serpent can have my sword, my daughter's hand in marriage and my kingdom when I die."

Soon, many brave knights came to the island to try and slay the sea serpent. Some had killed dragons before, but the sea serpent was much, much bigger. When most of them saw the sea serpent, they ran away.

The bravest ones tried to defeat it, but they only knew how to fight on land. Their armor was too heavy and they were soon gobbled up by the monstrous serpent.

At this time, a farmer and his wife lived on the island with their seven sons. The sons were all lively, active young men, apart from the youngest. He was small and thin and liked to dream about adventures as he sat at the fireside. His older brothers loved to tease and bully him.

When the family heard about the sea serpent, the youngest brother said "I can defeat it," very quietly. Everyone laughed at him. "You can't even hold a shield, or swing a sword!" said his brothers.

"I don't need a sword, or shield, to defeat the sea serpent," said the youngest brother, staring into the fire. The family didn't listen. They thought that the boy had got caught up in one of his own stories.

But the youngest brother was cleverer than he looked. When everyone had gone to bed and the fire had died down, he picked up a square of peat from the fire. Peat burns very slowly and the boy saw that there was still a tiny spark of flame in the middle of it.

The youngest brother took the peat and went out to the stable, where his father's horse stood. He got on the horse and galloped as fast as he could to the castle where the sea serpent waited. It was almost dawn when he reached a port near the castle. He found a small rowing boat and got in it, carrying only the peat.

Then, the youngest brother rowed as fast as he could out to the sea serpent, which was laying with its gigantic mouth half in the water. The sea serpent was sleeping and every so often it opened its mouth and yawned.

The youngest brother waited until the sea serpent yawned again and then rowed the boat right inside the sea serpent's mouth. Suddenly, the boat was floating down the sea serpent's throat at top speed, splashing and rocking. The boy held on tight until the boat came to rest in the sea serpent's belly.

It was very dark and smelly in the beast's stomach. The only light was the tiny flame from the lump of peat. The youngest brother blew gently on the flame and it slowly grew, until the belly was lit up with the fire. It was like a great, red cavern. Then he put the burning peat down next to a pile of wood from a ship that the sea serpent had swallowed. It soon caught flame and burned merrily.

The sea serpent felt the fire in its belly and woke up. Its stomach started to twist and shudder like an earthquake. The boy got back in the boat and rowed back towards the beast's mouth. As the serpent roared with pain, he rowed right out of its mouth again.

The sea serpent was burning up from inside. It snaked its head at the boat and tried to crush the boy in its jaws. Luckily, he managed to avoid its attacks and rowed as fast as he could towards the shore. With one last mighty roar, the sea serpent died and its head smashed back into the water.

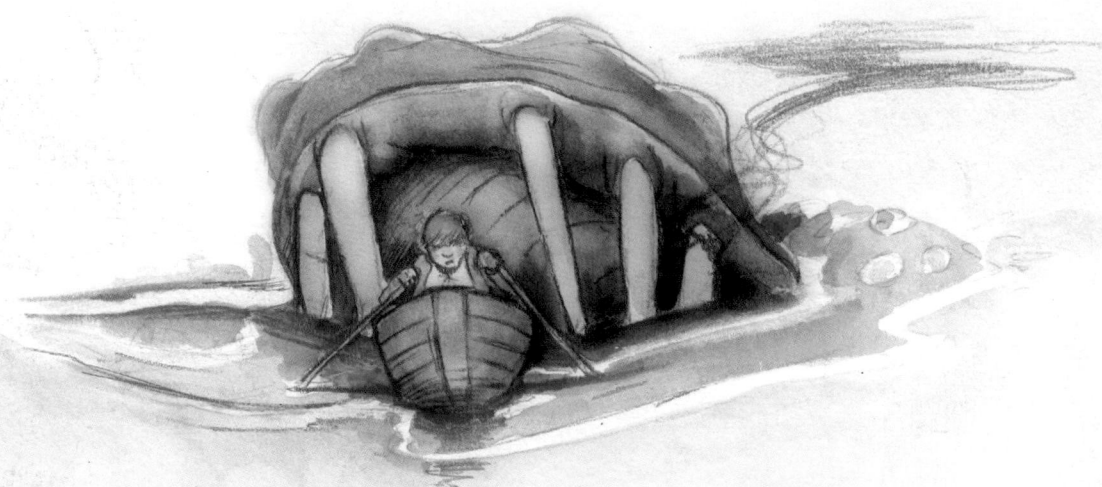

The wave carried the youngest brother all the way back to the port. When the people on the land saw what the youngest brother had done, they took him to the king and he was proclaimed a great hero.

The youngest brother married the king's daughter and took the king's sword. But he didn't forget his family. He invited them all to come and live in the castle with him and he made sure his throne was near a great fire, just like his place near the hearth at his old home. So the youngest brother, the princess and all their family lived happily ever after.

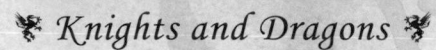

The Knight's Tower

Once there was a kind young man called Thomas, the youngest of three brothers. His two older brothers had both gone into the world to seek their fortunes. They were known far and wide as brave young men who fought monsters and rescued maidens.

Thomas longed to be a hero, just like his brothers, but he didn't know how. "If only I could find out what the secret of being a hero is," he thought, sadly.

One day, Thomas was walking along a forest path when he saw a strange old man who had fallen down in a puddle. Thomas helped him up. "In return for your kindness," said the old man, "I will answer any question you ask."

"How do I become a hero?" asked Thomas.

The old man smiled crookedly. "There is only one person who can tell you that," he said. "You must ask the knight who lives at the top of the tall tower, in the depths of the woods."

Thomas was puzzled by the old man's words, but he thanked him anyway and then set off into the woods. He hadn't gone far before he heard a strange, whining sound. Thomas followed the sound, which seemed to be coming from a clearing near the trees.

Thomas reached the clearing, and found a wolf that was whining. Thomas was about to run away, when he saw that the wolf had a thorn in its paw. "If I help it, it may try to bite me," thought Thomas, but he plucked the thorn from the wolf's paw any way.

"Thank you, stranger," said the wolf, in a soft voice. "Can I help you?"

"I'm looking for the knight's tower," said Thomas.

"I will show you the way," said the wolf. Thomas followed the wolf deep into the forest. "This is as far as I will go," the wolf said and disappeared back into the woods.

Thomas carried on walking, until he heard another sound. It was a great groaning and growling. Pushing through the trees, Thomas found a great brown bear that had caught its paw under a fallen tree. "If I help it, it may chase me when it's free," thought Thomas. But he helped the bear to pull it's paw out any way.

Instead of attacking Thomas, the bear asked, "What can I do for you?" Thomas told him about the knight's tower. "I will carry you to the tower," said the bear. "Climb on my back."

Thomas climbed on the bear's back. It ran through the forest until it reached a tower that was so high above the trees, its top was lost in the clouds.

The bear ran back into the forest while Thomas looked all around the tower. He saw that it had no door, or windows. It was impossible to get inside.

Thomas heard a low, rumbling roar. Following the sound, Thomas found a great, green dragon. It had been caught in a landslide and one of its wings was trapped under a big pile of rocks. "If I help the dragon, it will surely eat me," thought Thomas. But the dragon seemed so sad and hurt, that Thomas couldn't leave it. He took rocks off the dragon's wing, until it was free again.

The dragon reared up and flapped its wings and Thomas was afraid that it would heat him up. But the dragon asked, "How may I thank you?" Thomas explained about the knight's tower.

"Climb on my back," said the dragon. Thomas was scared, but he did as the dragon suggested. Thomas clung on to the dragon's neck and it flew up into the clouds. Above the clouds, Thomas saw a small ledge and a door at the top of the tower. The dragon flew to the ledge and Thomas stepped onto it.

The door was opened by a knight in gleaming armor. He invited Thomas into the tower. "Great knight," asked Thomas, "how can I become a hero?"

"A hero has kindness," said the knight. "Did you help the wolf in the woods?"
"Yes," said Thomas.

"A hero has spirit," said the knight. "Did you ride the bear?"
"Yes," said Thomas.
"And, most of all, a hero has courage," said the knight, "did you fly up here with the dragon?"
"I did," said Thomas.

 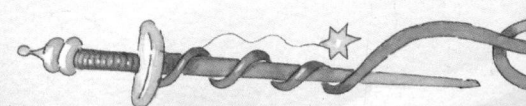

"Then you are a hero already," the knight said. "At the bottom of the tower, you will find gifts fit for a hero."

The dragon flew Thomas back down to the bottom of the tower. A proud, black horse and a shining suit of armor were waiting for him.

Thomas put the suit of armor on and rode the black horse through the forest to seek his fortune. After many adventures, Thomas made his fortune and became the greatest hero in the land and lived happily ever after.

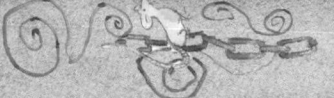 
The Troll Knight

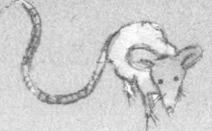

Once upon a time, a knight called Sir Bedwin lived in a white castle. Sir Bedwin rode a pure white horse and his armor always gleamed. Every day, the king and his daughter, the princess, passed Sir Bedwin's castle. Sir Bedwin would always gallop out and salute them, holding his shining sword high in the air. Sir Bedwin was very proud of his horse, his armor and his castle.

One day, Sir Bedwin was galloping past the lake near his castle when he came upon an old woman. She was bent and ugly. She had a warty nose and crooked teeth and a humped back.

"Be off with you," said Sir Bedwin sternly, getting down from his horse. "Don't you know that the king is passing by soon? He won't want to see an old hag like you!"

The old woman was a witch. "How dare you speak to me in that way?" she shrieked. "Let's see how you like being ugly," She raised her hands and muttered a powerful spell.

Sir Bedwin felt his body growing larger. His armor popped off and flew in all directions. His horse ran away in fright. Sir Bedwin looked at himself in the lake and found he was a hairy, blue-grey troll. His arms were long and his fingers ended in claws. He had a huge nose and giant yellow teeth. And his eyes were as big and round as dinner plates.

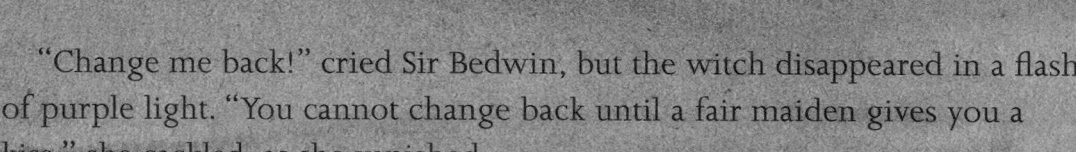

"Change me back!" cried Sir Bedwin, but the witch disappeared in a flash of purple light. "You cannot change back until a fair maiden gives you a kiss," she cackled, as she vanished.

Sir Bedwin walked back to his castle in anger. "Look at what has happened to me," he called to his knights.

But when they saw him, they charged at him, yelling. "Slay the troll." Sir Bedwin tried to run away, but the knights threw thick chains around him and dragged him to the castle dungeons.

"Sir Bedwin will deal with you later," they told him. No matter how many times he tried to explain about the witch's curse, they wouldn't listen.

It was miserable in the dungeon. Two knights guarded Sir Bedwin all the time and the only other creatures he saw were the mice that ran across his prison cell. Sir Bedwin gave the mice scraps of his food. "At least you're not afraid of me," he said to them.

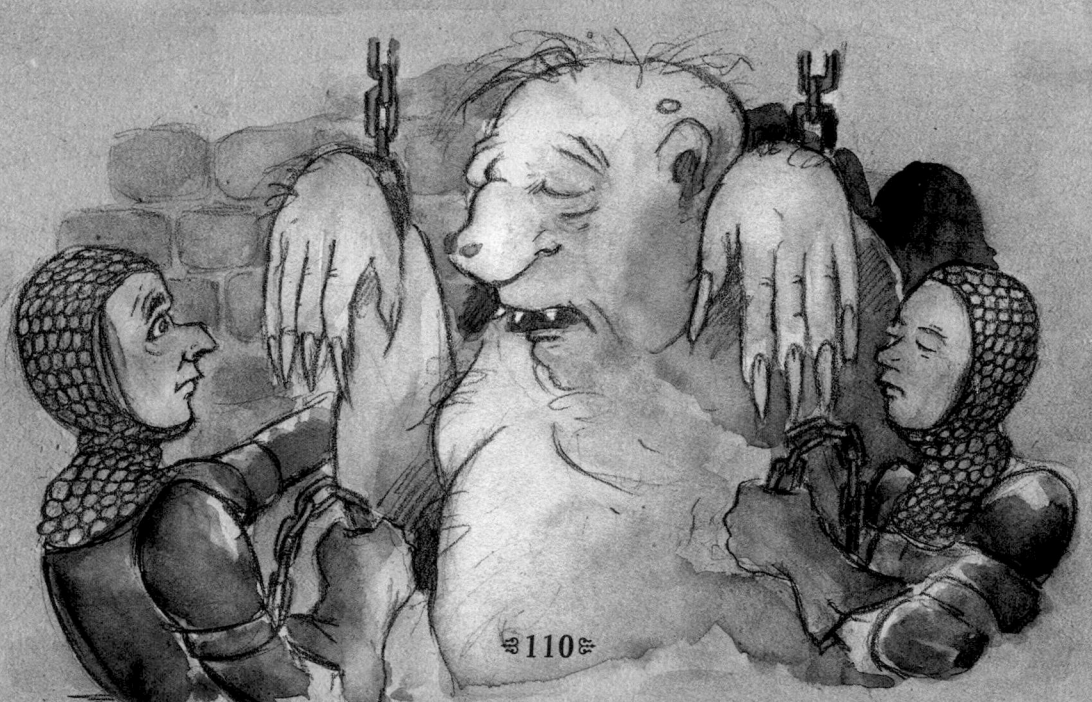

"Where is Sir Bedwin?" said one of the knights on guard, one day.

"I'm glad he's not here," said the other knight. "He makes us polish and clean everywhere in the castle. While he is gone, we can enjoy ourselves." Sir Bedwin sighed. He hadn't realised that he had been so cruel to his knights.

One moonlit night, Sir Bedwin was woken by a tiny tapping on his big troll nose. It was one of the mice. It pointed to the wooden door and Sir Bedwin saw that the mice had gnawed through the hinges. He could finally escape.

"Thank you, my friends," said Sir Bedwin, softly, as he sneaked past the snoring guards and out of the castle.

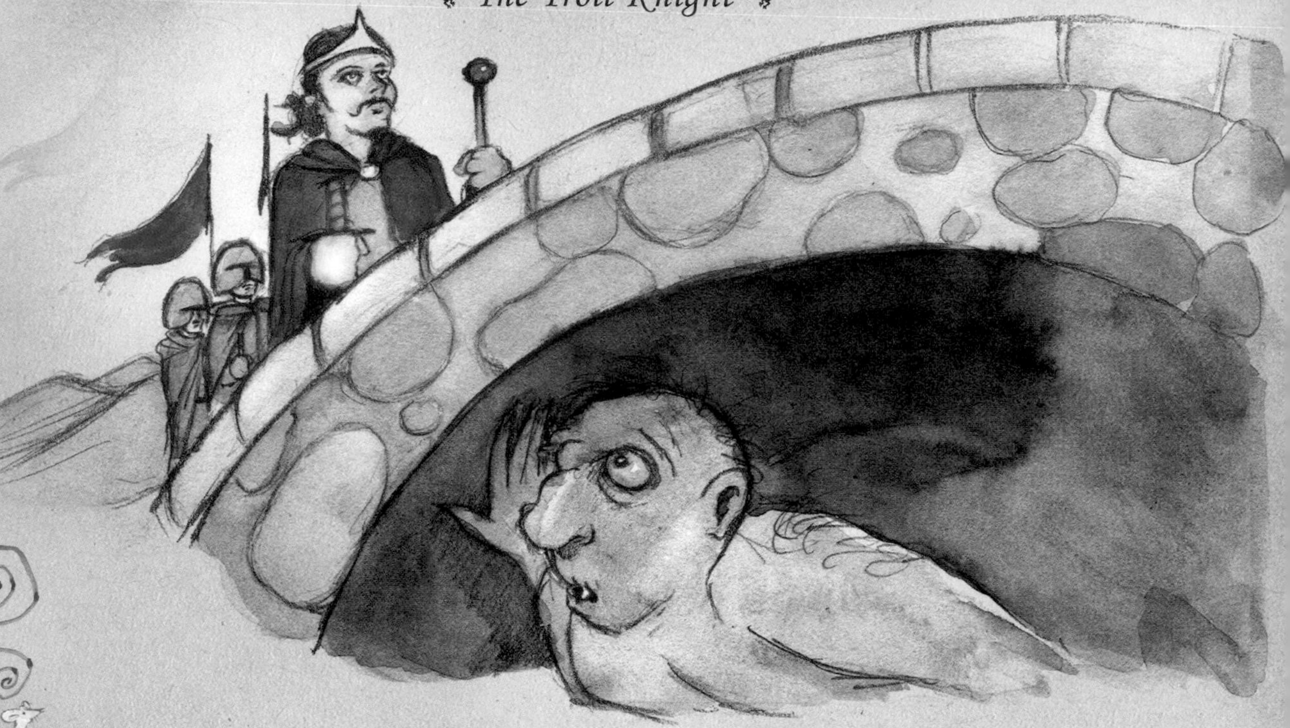

But life in the world outside the castle was hardly any better. Nobody wanted to be friends with a troll. Of course, no fair maiden would even go near him, so he could never get the kiss that would restore his true shape.

Sir Bedwin wandered far and wide, until he found himself in a land to the west of his kingdom, ruled by an evil emperor.

As the emperor and his men crossed a bridge one day, Sir Bedwin hid under a nearby bridge and listened to what they were saying. "Soon we will attack the land to the east," said the emperor. "Then the king's castle will be mine."

"I must tell my king," gasped Sir Bedwin. He started the long journey back to his kingdom.

Winter had covered the land in snow and the journey was cold and hard. The emperor's army were marching only a day behind him. But he struggled on, until he saw the towers of the king's castle in front of him.

"I have important news for the king," he said to the sentries at the gate. But they wouldn't listen. They drove him away with their weapons.

Sir Bedwin was so angry, he almost roared in rage. But he thought of a plan. That night, when nobody could see him, he used his great ogre's claws to climb the stone walls of the castle. It was a long, difficult climb, but eventually Sir Bedwin reached the window of the tallest tower and slipped in. The king and the princess were there, surrounded by their royal guards.

"Sire," said Sir Bedwin, "your kingdom is in grave danger."
The guards rushed at Sir Bedwin to strike him, but the wise king stopped them. "Let us hear what this creature has to say," the king said.

Sir Bedwin explained about the emperor's army. The king sent out scouts and found that Sir Bedwin was telling the truth. The army wasn't far behind, but the king had enough time to pull up the drawbridge and defend the castle from the army. There was a great siege, but after many days, the evil emperor's army was defeated.

"You saved the kingdom," said the king to Sir Bedwin. "What would you like in return?"
"I don't want anything," said Sir Bedwin. "It is enough to know that the kingdom is safe."

When she heard this, the king's daughter was so grateful that she stood on tiptoe and kissed Sir Bedwin on the end of his huge troll's nose.

Sir Bedwin felt himself begin to grow smaller. His claws turned back into hands, and his nose and eyes shrank. He was human again. Everyone in the palace was amazed.

Sir Bedwin and the princess fell in love and were married. Years later, Sir Bedwin became king and ruled the land wisely. He made sure that he never judged anybody on their appearance and he was never rude to a witch again.

The Fire Dragon

Once upon a time, there was a little village near a sea. It was a quiet, sleepy place, until a dragon decided to make its home in a nearby cliff.

This dragon was bright red and seemed to glow from inside like hot coals. When it opened its mouth to roar, great flames shot out and it left scorching footprints wherever it walked.

Unless the villagers piled up coal outside the dragon's lair for it to eat, it would fly over the town, setting fire to buildings and scorching the fields. There were no knights in the village and when the villagers sent a messenger to the king, he replied that all his knights were busy in foreign lands.

A miller's son lived in the old mill by the deep, wide river that ran through the village. "What can we do?" he asked his grandfather, who sat in a chair by the fire. "Soon, the dragon will destroy the whole village."

"Only one thing can destroy a fire dragon," said his grandfather, pouring a little water on the fire so it hissed. "A water dragon. But the water dragons are proud and mighty and live in the deep ocean. They don't like humans. I don't think they will help us."

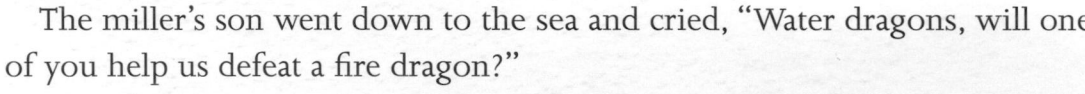 
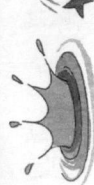

The miller's son went down to the sea and cried, "Water dragons, will one of you help us defeat a fire dragon?"

A great head reared out of the water, towering high over the miller's son. It was a dragon whose body shimmered and flowed like the water itself. "Do not disturb us," said the water dragon. "We hate fire dragons as much as we have no love for humans."

"All these people will die if you don't help us," said the miller's son. "I will help you only if you can prove to me that humans are worth saving," said the water dragon. "Show me a marvel that humans have made." "If only we had a great castle, or a magic ring, or a golden statue," thought the miller's son. "But our village is a poor one. We have nothing to show the dragon."

As he thought, he tore off a chunk of bread to eat.

"What is that?" asked the water dragon.

"This?" said the miller's son. "This is bread."

The water dragon had never seen bread before. The miller's son explained how the farmer grew the seed and harvested the crop. He told the dragon how his father milled it into flour and how the village baker made it into dough which rose in the oven to become bread.

"Humans make this together?" asked the water dragon. "For all our strength and power, no dragon has ever worked with another to make anything so good and useful. This bread is a marvel. I will help you."

The water dragon dived back down into the water and, for a moment, the miller's son thought it had gone. But the water dragon shot out of the sea, like a gigantic wave. It rushed down the river into the village, faster than the miller's son could run.

The fire dragon had come down from its nest. When it saw the water dragon in the river, it gave a horrible roar and pounced on it and a great battle began. The water dragon tried to drench the fire dragon, to put out its flame, but the fire dragon breathed its fierce flame on the water dragon.

They twisted and turned like great snakes in the water and, wherever fire touched water, there was a loud hissing sound. All the villagers came to watch the battle, but the river was covered in clouds of steam and smoke.

The fire dragon dragged the water dragon to the river bank. On land, the water dragon's powers were weaker and he couldn't fight back. As the fire dragon leaned down to bite the water dragon, the water dragon gave a loud cry.

Down the river streamed all the other water dragons, in a crash of foam and spray. They pulled the fire dragon off the water dragon and plunged him deep into the river, until the dragon's fire went out. The fire dragon was swept out to sea, never to return.

The miller's son tried to thank the water dragons, but they had already returned to the sea.

So the miller's son and everyone else in the village, was free from the fire dragon and they all lived happily and peacefully ever after.

The Jester's Quest

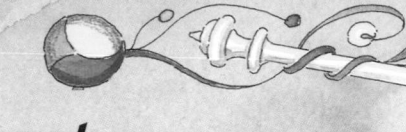

Once upon a time, there was an evil green dragon who lived in a cave in the mountains. This dragon flew around the kingdom, eating sheep, scaring children and sometimes even gobbling up a villager, or two.

The queen summoned all the knights of the castle to appear in her Great Hall. "Is there any one of you who is brave enough to fight the dragon?"

But all the knights stayed silent. They were old and cowardly and they had no wish to fight the dragon.

The queen's jester, sitting at the foot of her throne, laughed at them. "They're no braver than a crowd of kittens, Your Majesty!" This jester was the queen's favourite. He loved to laugh and joke and wave his stick and shake his yellow and red cap covered with bells.

"Then I will choose one of you at random," said the queen. "I make a solemn oath that whomever's name is picked will fight the dragon." All the knight's names were put in a silver box and one was drawn out. The queen announced the name in a loud voice. "The one who is going to fight the dragon is the jester."

The hall fell silent as the jester stepped forward. "But I'm not a knight, Your Majesty," the jester said. "This is some kind of mistake,"

"Nevertheless!" said the queen sternly. "You will leave tomorrow to fight the dragon."

On the first night of his journey, the jester stayed at a tavern near a large stone circle. He entertained the people there with acrobatics, but he asked for no payment. Instead, he asked the people of the tavern to cover the stones of the circle with white paint. They were puzzled, but did as he asked.

Next, the jester passed through a rocky ravine filled with enormous boulders. The people came from miles around to hear his jokes but, instead of asking for money, he asked the people to roll a gigantic boulder down the ravine, where it broke in two.

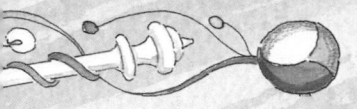 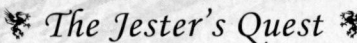
Finally, the jester came to a small village at the bottom of the dragon's mountain. The people here were grim and wary but, nevertheless, they laughed at his stories and his juggling tricks. "Give me no money," said the jester. "Instead, please dig a deep round hole and then dig three triangular holes into the side of it." The villagers were puzzled, but they agreed to do as the jester asked.

The jester said goodbye to them and journeyed all the way up the cold, dark mountain to the dragon's cave. At the entrance to the cave, the jester was almost too scared to go in. "It's no worse than performing in front of the queen," he thought and although this was far from true, it gave him the courage to enter the cave.

Inside, the dragon was crouched on its treasure, growling and spitting and gouging great scratches into the rock with its long claws. "Another knight to challenge me," roared the dragon. "Come here, so I can eat you." The dragon batted at the jester and picked him up in his claws, like a cat picks up a mouse.

"Wait, oh mighty dragon," squeaked the jester. "I'm not a knight. I am here on behalf of the Great Dragon. He wants to challenge you to a fight." "The Great Dragon? I've never heard of him," roared the dragon. But it didn't eat the jester.

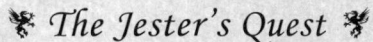

"The Great Dragon wants to find out if you are as strong as he is," the jester said. "That is, if you're brave enough."

The dragon roared like a furnace and huge blasts of flame shot from its nostrils. "Take me to this so-called Great Dragon," said the dragon.

The jester led the dragon down the mountain, to the place where the villagers had dug the big hole. It was so big, the dragon could almost fit in it. "Oh, look," said the jester. "Here is one of the Great Dragon's footprints. He can't be far."

The dragon looked surprised. "I don't care how big he is, I'll beat him."

So the jester took the dragon to the ravine, where he saw the mighty boulder that was smashed in two. "Look," said the jester. "The Great Dragon eats boulders like this for breakfast. He must have crunched this one up then spat it out, because it's too small."

For the first time, the dragon seemed nervous. "He certainly sounds very fierce," it growled.

Then the jester and the dragon reached the stone circle that the local people had painted white. "Ah," said the jester, as the dragon wandered around the circle, looking at the huge stones. "This is an old set of the Great Dragon's teeth! He grows a new set every year. This one must be from a few years back, as they're quite small compared to his new set. In fact, I think I see the Great Dragon in the distance."

This was too much for the dragon. It yelped in fright and flew away in fear to a far-off land, where it hoped the Great Dragon would never find it.

The jester chuckled and travelled back to the dragon's empty cave. He took its treasure and brought it back to the palace. All the knights were very surprised and the queen was exceedingly grateful.

"There's one thing I don't understand, Your Majesty," said the jester. "Who put my name in the silver box in the first place?"

"Why, it must have been someone who knew you were the bravest, cleverest man in the castle," said the queen, smiling secretly to herself.

The jester took his treasure away, but he didn't stop jesting. He became the only jester in the land who carried a stick made of gold and wore a silver cap with real gold bells.

The Knight of the Golden Lion

Once upon a time, a king had a son called Prince Malcolm. The prince was small and thin and he wasn't very good at royal sports. When he tried falconry, he got bitten by the falcons. When he tried hunting, he was chased by wolves. He tried archery, but he nearly shot himself in the foot. Nothing seemed to work for him.

But Prince Malcolm loved to watch jousting tournaments, where two knights on horseback charged at each other with lances and tried to knock each other to the ground. It was very fast and very dangerous, but the prince wished he could join in.

Prince Malcolm went to his father, the king. "How can I become a great knight?" he asked him.

"Go to the sorceress who lives in the lonely stone house on the hill," said the king. "She will surely be able to help you."

Prince Malcolm journeyed to the lonely stone house, expecting to meet an old hag. But the sorceress was a beautiful girl, no older than he was.

"I can help, if you really want it," said the sorceress. "But magic comes with its own price. You won't know what it is until you are required to pay. Do you still want to be a great knight?"

"Oh, yes!" said Prince Malcolm. So the sorceress gathered her potions and threw them into the eerie green fire in the middle of the room. "Reach into the fire," the sorceress said. Prince Malcolm reached in – it wasn't hot! He pulled out a golden lance. He thanked the sorceress and took the lance back to the castle.

Prince Malcolm entered the very next tournament and found that the golden lance was enchanted. As he galloped towards the enemy knights, it seemed to find its target on its own. Soon, everyone was cheering Prince Malcolm, but nobody knew the secret of the golden lance.

As the prince was readying his horse for the next tournament, a strange knight came riding up. The knight wore gold armor that sparkled in the sun. His helmet was shaped like a lion's head, over his stern, bearded face.

 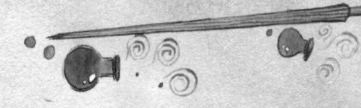
Strangest of all, he wasn't riding a horse. He was riding a great, shaggy lion, which lifted its head and roared loud enough to scare all the horses.

"I am the knight of the golden lion," cried the knight. "Who here will challenge me?"

The king checked the jousting rules anxiously. "There's nothing in the rules that says a knight on a lion can't compete," he told his knights. "You may accept his challenge."

One after another, the king's knights lined up and charged at the knight of the golden lion. His ferocious lion terrified the horses, so that they couldn't gallop straight. The knight of the golden lion batted their lances away like straws and knocked them all down.

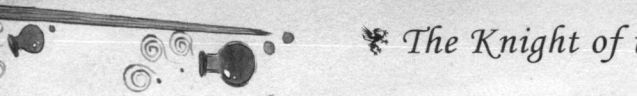
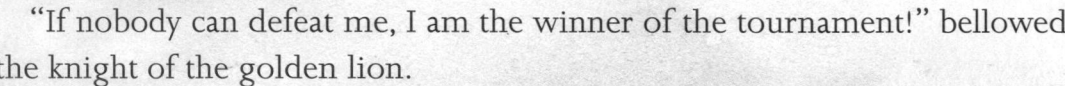

"If nobody can defeat me, I am the winner of the tournament!" bellowed the knight of the golden lion.

"Wait," said Prince Malcolm in a small voice. "I will challenge you at dawn tomorrow."

That evening, Prince Malcolm visited the sorceress. She chanted into her fire, until strange images appeared.

"The knight draws his power from his golden helmet," said the sorceress. "Only golden magic can defeat golden magic. You must aim your lance at the helmet. When it touches it, both the lance and the helmet will disappear."

"But without the lance, I can't win the tournament," said Prince Malcolm in dismay.

"I told you there would be a price," said the sorceress.

Before the sun came up the next morning, the prince was ready and waiting. He put his armor on, saddled his horse and took up his lance. As the sun came over the hills, the knight of the golden lion appeared on his shaggy beast. "Do you still dare challenge me?" growled the knight. Prince Malcolm nodded. He was too nervous to speak.

In front of the watching crowd, the prince and the knight galloped towards each other. The prince's horse was brave and kept a straight path towards the knight.

The ground seemed to flash past the prince. He tried to aim the golden lance at the knight's helmet, but it resisted. It wanted to hit the knight in the chest.

With all his strength, Prince Malcolm forced the golden lance up. It just caught the crest of the helmet and pushed it to the ground.

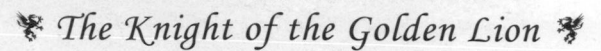 
The knight of the golden lion changed. Suddenly, his armor was rusty steel. His mighty lion became a regular horse and he was no bigger, or stronger looking stranger looking than Prince Malcolm. "It's not fair!" cried the knight. "But I'm still not beaten. You have one last chance to knock me down, or I win this tournament."

Prince Malcolm took a normal wooden lance from the sorceress, who was watching. "Are you going to tell me that the golden lance wasn't magical at all?" asked the prince. "Maybe it was your cunning trick and I had the strength I needed to beat the knight of the golden lion all along?"

"No," said the sorceress. "The lance really was magic."

"Ah," said Prince Malcolm. "Then I truly have no hope."

The sorceress smiled at him and kissed him on the cheek. "I think you can do it," she said.

Dazed, embarrassed and pleased, the prince faced the knight one last time. The wooden lance was heavy and awkward, but he held it tightly. As his horse thundered towards the knight, he tilted it down onto the knight's shield. The lance splintered and the knight of the golden lion shook, then wobbled, then toppled to the ground, cursing.

The crowd rose to their feet and cheered and the king awarded Prince Malcolm the title of 'Champion of the tournament'.

Prince Malcolm married the sorceress soon after. Together, they lived happily ever after and Prince Malcolm became a great and powerful knight.

Sir Richard and the Red Knight

Once upon a time, a brave knight called Sir Richard lived in a castle, all on his own. Sir Richard was a great warrior, but he was proud and haughty. He had no friends to visit him in his castle and he lived a lonely life.

One day, there was a great thump on the castle gate. "Let me in!" a deep voice cried. "I am the Red Knight!"

Sir Richard opened the gate and saw a tremendous sight. It was a man dressed in red armor. Sir Richard was tall, but this man was even taller. He towered over Sir Richard. The Red Knight had a long red beard and red hair and even his eyes seemed to flame and glow.

"Make way, Sir Richard," said the Red Knight, stepping into the empty courtyard of the castle. "I like the look of your castle. I claim it as my own."

"Never!" cried Sir Richard, drawing his long sword. "I challenge you to a duel. If you win, you may take my castle. If you lose, you must leave, never to return."

"Agreed," said the Red Knight and he drew his great, red sword, which glinted dangerously. Sir Richard also drew his sword and the two knights began to fight.

Sir Richard had never fought anyone like the Red Knight before. All his sword blows bounced off the knight's red armor. Even though the Red Knight was so big, he was also very fast. Sir Richard fought bravely, but the Red Knight struck the sword from Sir Richard's hands and threw him to the ground.

Sir Richard had no choice, but to leave his beloved castle with nothing more than the clothes on his back and his sword. He staggered into the woods below the castle, weary and sad.

Day after day, Sir Richard wandered through the woods. He slept under the trees, with a rock for a pillow. Soon, his clothes became tattered and worn and his face grew pinched and pale.

One day, when he had gathered up a small pile of nuts and berries to eat, he heard someone approach. It was a dirty-looking old beggar. "Please," said the beggar, "can you spare some of your food?"

Sir Richard took pity on the poor man and shared his tiny meal. "Thank you," said the beggar. "Let's travel the land together."
Sir Richard agreed and soon he found it was much easier to find food in the forest when there were two people to look.

Some time later, Sir Richard and the beggar found a horse in a clearing. It was the noblest horse the knight had ever seen. Its coat was a silky white and its head was held high. But it was limping from a wound to its front leg.

Sir Richard spoke softly to the horse and bound its leg with a scrap torn from his clothes. "You can join us," he said to the horse and we will take care of you." Sir Richard thought of all the horses he had kept in his stables in the castle and wished he had taken better care of them. "I know what it's like to be cold and hungry now," Sir Richard thought.

As the days passed by, the horse's leg began to get better and before long, it was cantering around happily and nibbling the grass.

One day, as Sir Richard, the beggar and the horse made their way through the woods, they heard a desperate roar. Sir Richard followed the sound and found a great brown bear. One of its paws was caught in a cruel trap. The bear turned its head to Sir Richard and he saw so much pain in its eyes, that he felt he had to help.

Carefully, Sir Richard walked up to the bear. It did not attack him, but only groaned louder. Sir Richard prised open the jaws of the trap with all his might. The bear pulled its paw out of the trap. With a grateful look, it lumbered off into the deep forest.

"That cruel trap must have been set by the Red Knight," said Sir Richard to the beggar. "I wish I could defeat him and win my castle back."

"Perhaps you can," said the beggar. "I was once a great magician before the Red Knight cheated me out of all my riches. I still have some magic left." The beggar took Sir Richard's old sword and spoke some strange words over it. The sword glowed with an eerie power.
"Now the sword will pierce the Red Knight's armor," said the beggar.

So Sir Richard made the long journey back to his castle, riding on the white horse. He banged on the gate, just as the Red Knight had done.

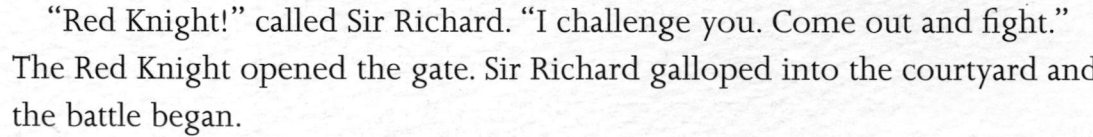

"Red Knight!" called Sir Richard. "I challenge you. Come out and fight." The Red Knight opened the gate. Sir Richard galloped into the courtyard and the battle began.

The Red Knight was quick, but Sir Richard was on horseback this time and the horse was quicker than the Red Knight. Sir Richard was able to deal the Red Knight some powerful blows with his enchanted sword.

Just when it looked like Sir Richard would beat him, the Red Knight raised his arms and chanted a spell. Sir Richard found himself pulled off the horse. "Now I will kill you!" cried the Red Knight, raising his sword to chop off Sir Richard's head.

Before he could bring the sword down, the Red Knight was knocked over by something huge and brown. It was the bear that Sir Richard had saved from the trap. Together, Sir Richard and the bear drove the Red Knight out of the castle. The Red Knight ran down the hill and far away, defeated at last.

In a flash, the bear turned into a noble knight. "I was cursed by the Red Knight," he said, "but now we have broken his power forever."

So Sir Richard reclaimed his castle at last. He invited the knight and the beggar magician to live with him and the white horse was given a warm stable and all the hay it could eat. With his new friends around him, Sir Richard was never lonely again.

Sir Gawaine and the Green Knight

It was Christmas in the castle of Camelot. King Arthur and his knights were celebrating with a great feast. Fires flickered and the tables groaned under the weight of the food. All the knights and their ladies were laughing and joking.

Suddenly, the door of the Great Hall flew open and a giant knight rode in. He was covered in green armor. His eyes seemed to glow like emeralds. His beard was like a tangle of twigs and leaves. Even his horses coat was a deep, mossy green. He carried a sharp axe made of some strange green metal. It was almost as big as he was. Bright holly berries grew around the handle.

King Arthur and his knights sat in silence as the strange knight said, "I challenge one of you to a battle to the death. You must strike me first. Then you must promise that I will have a chance to strike you back. Are any of you beardless little boys brave enough to fight me?"

"Sir Gawaine was the most courageous of Arthur's knights. He rose to his feet. "I accept." he said. So, the green knight got off his horse.

Sir Gawaine swung his sword and chopped at the the green knight's head

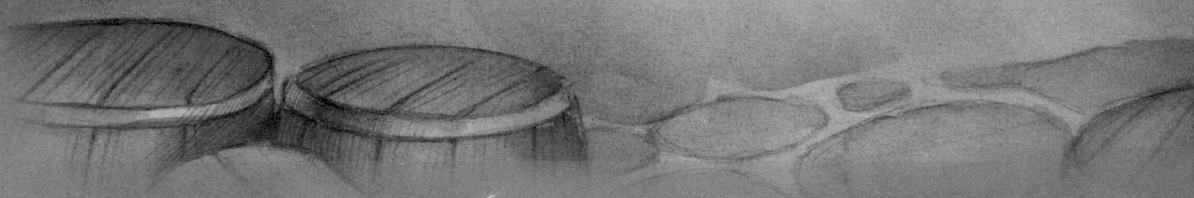

He did not know that the strange knight was enchanted and instead of falling over, the green knight calmly picked up his head.

"In a year and a day," said the head, "you must promise to find me in the green chapel. It will only appear to you if you do not hunt, or kill. Then it will be my turn to strike you." The green knight got on his horse and thundered out of the castle, carrying his head.

"I must find the green chapel," Sir Gawaine said, "And let the green knight strike me with his axe."

"But he'll kill you," said King Arthur.

"A promise is a promise," said Sir Gawaine, sadly. "A knight always keeps his word."

Nobody in Camelot had ever heard of the green chapel. So Sir Gawaine rode across England all through spring and summer, trying to find it.

As the leaves started to fall from the trees, Sir Gawaine rode into an old, dark forest. In those days, there were still many wild and terrible creatures roaming the forest. Sir Gawaine had to fight off twisting green dragons that nested in the roots of trees. He scared wolves away with fire. He even had to fend off the wild men of the woods, who were half-tree, half-man. But he did not hunt, or kill any wild animal, because he knew that if he did, he would never enter the green chapel.

After many adventures, Sir Gawaine came to a great mansion in the middle of the forest. A friendly, red-cheeked man opened the door to him. Sir Gawaine asked if he had heard of the green chapel.

"I am Sir Bertilak," the man said. "The green chapel is a short distance away. Stay with us until the year is done. All I ask is that you come hunting with me."

Sir Bertilak's wife was a beautiful lady. "Fetch me a deer, Sir Gawaine and prove you are the best knight in the land," she said.

So, the next day, Sir Gawaine went hunting with Sir Bertilak. Sir Gawaine saw a beautiful deer. But Sir Gawaine knew he could not kill it, or he would never enter the green chapel. He pretended to get his arrows ready and the deer ran off.

"Fetch me a boar," said Sir Bertilak's wife on the second day.

Sir Gawaine found a huge wild boar, deep in the forest. It charged with its deadly tusks, but Sir Gawaine batted it away with his sword and it disappeared back into the forest.
"There is a red fox in the wood," Sir Bertilak's wife said on the third day. "Anyone who wears its skin will be safe from axe blows."

Sir Bertilak and Sir Gawaine went into the forest and found the fox drinking at a pool. This time, Sir Gawaine aimed his bow and, by mistake, he shot an arrow at the fox, but it swiftly ran away.

The next day, it was a year and a day since Sir Gawaine's promise. He rode to the green chapel and found a high sheet of rock, covered in ivy.
Sir Gawaine placed his hand on the rock and it parted, letting him inside.

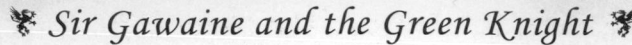

Sir Gawaine and the Green Knight

The green chapel was a cavern, deep in the earth. Its walls sparkled with emeralds and deep tree roots. The green knight was waiting for him. His head was back on his shoulders.

"Lay your head down on this stone," boomed the green knight, "and I'll strike my blow."

Trembling, Sir Gawaine knelt down and put his head on the cold stone. The green knight brought down the axe–right to the edge of Gawaine's neck. "A bad stroke," said the green knight. "Let me try again." He brought the axe down a second time and stopped it once more on Gawaine's neck. "One last time," said the green knight. "And this time, I will strike."

The green knight brought the axe down for a third time. It just grazed Sir Gawaine's neck, leaving a tiny mark.

"Now you have struck me and the bargain is complete!" shouted Sir Gawaine. "Let's fight like men." He drew his sword. But the green knight was laughing.

"I am Sir Bertilak," said the green knight. "Or rather, he is me. I am the guardian of the enchanted forest. I decided to test your trustworthiness by seeing whether you would hunt my precious wild animals. The first and second times, you did not. On the third time, you shot an arrow at my fox. That is why my third strike touched your neck. But you have proved your goodness. You didn't break your promise, even though you thought it meant certain death. Arthur's knights are truly the greatest in the land."

Sir Gawaine rode home, amazed to have survived. When he told King Arthur and his knights about his adventure, they all decided to wear green ribbons, so that none of them would forget Sir Gawaine's courage, or the story of the green knight.

 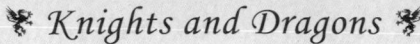 

The Ice Knight

Once upon a time, there were two brothers called Giles and Roderick. They loved to play with wooden swords and dreamed of growing up to be noble knights. Giles was steady and reliable, but Roderick was sharp-eyed and adventurous.

When it was time for them to leave home, the brothers journeyed in different directions. "We will meet again when we have made our fortunes," they said, shaking hands.

Giles followed the road into a valley. He hadn't been travelling long before he saw a group of robbers. They were attacking a man on horseback. Drawing his sword, Giles ran at the robbers and drove them all away.

The man on the horse was a noble prince. "You're a brave man, you can be my squire," he said to Giles.

Life was hard for Giles. He had to run errands for all the brave knights in the prince's service. But he learned how to fence and how to joust. It took a long time, but eventually he could fight better than any knight.

 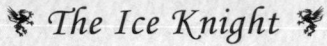 

Meanwhile, Roderick followed a different path. He had heard a legend of a great northern enchanter who was more powerful than any in the land. So Roderick travelled far to the north, to the lands of endless snow, until he found the enchanter's castle which was made of ice. Roderick went inside and found the enchanter on an ice throne, surrounded by blue-eyed snow leopards.

"I will work hard if you will let me serve you," Roderick said. "You can become a knight straight away," said the enchanter. "Only fools work hard." The enchanter cast a spell, and Roderick found himself in a chilly suit of armor that reflected the pale sun like glass.

The enchanter placed an amulet in the armor's chestplate. "This will give you great powers over snow and ice," he said.

Lastly, the enchanter pulled a great shard of ice from the palace and cast a spell over it. It became a great ice-sword which he gave to Roderick. "Now you are my Ice Knight," said the enchanter. "You must guard my castle from all intruders."

Roderick went to shake the enchanter's hand, but the enchanter moved away. "A human touch means death to me," he said.

Soon, Roderick found that he no longer felt the cold. In fact, the longer Roderick guarded the ice palace, the less he could feel in his heart.

 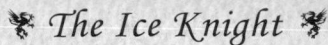 

One day, Giles prince told his knights about the enchanter. "This evil man wants to cover all the land in ice. He must be stopped. Who will challenge him for me?" Giles volunteered to go to the north and fight.

When Giles finished the weary journey to the far north, he found the ice castle. Roderick was outside guarding it. He stood as still as an icicle.

When Giles saw his brother, he was overjoyed. But Roderick had forgotten how to feel. "You shall not enter my master's castle," said Roderick. He swung his ice sword at his brother. Giles raised his sword to block it and they began to fight.

Roderick summoned shards of ice and a frozen wind to drive Giles back. But Giles swung his sword and knocked the amulet from the Ice Knight's chest. Now Roderick could not summon snow and ice against his brother. He was forced to use his sword to fight.

Because the ice knight had not worked as hard as his brother, he tired more easily. Soon, Roderick stumbled and fell into the snow. Instead of striking him down, Giles helped his brother to his feet.

The Ice Knight was amazed. "You could have defeated me. Why did you help me?" he asked.

"Because you are still my brother and I love you," said Giles.

Roderick felt his heart melting and all the warmth returning to his body. "I have been bewitched all this time. Let's defeat the enchanter together!" he cried.

They entered the palace to find their way blocked by the snow leopards. "We have been enslaved by the enchanter," said the leader of the snow leopards. "We will fight with you for our freedom."

Inside, the enchanter was waiting for them. "Traitor!" he cried to Roderick.

Shards of ice formed into sparkling, spiky ice-men, but Giles and Roderick shattered them all with their swords.

The enchanter tried to run, but the growling snow leopards blocked his escape. Giles ran to the enchanter and grabbed him by the arm.

At Giles' warm touch, the enchanter began to melt, until he was nothing more than a puddle on the floor! Around him, the ice castle shook. It began to collapse into the snow. As the castle disappeared, the snow leopards ran away to freedom.

The brothers made the long journey home, weary but happy to be together again. When they returned, the prince knighted both brothers. Together, Sir Giles and Sir Roderick defended the kingdom from danger and lived happily ever after.